# THE GAY HAUNT

by

I0665130

Victor J. Banis

**The Borgo Press**
**An Imprint of Wildside Press**

MMVII

SECOND EDITION

# CONTENTS

## CHAPTER ONE

The first time, he came for cocktails. I suppose that should not have seemed too surprising. After all, there were a dozen other people there for the same purpose and, also, ostensibly to meet my *fiancée*, Margo Sellers, although most of them had known her longer than I had.

So the addition of another male guest, even an unexpected one, shouldn't have been altogether alarming. There's usually at least one uninvited guest at every such function. However, there is nothing quite so likely to create a sensation at a cocktail party as the appearance of a male guest in the raw.

For one thing, there is the breach of etiquette to consider. It implies either a gauche ignorance on the part of the guest, or inadequate information on the part of the host. For another thing, it tends to discomfort the other guests who, at the very least, are certain to feel overdressed.

"Of all the nerve," I thought angrily, staring in astonishment at the naked body posed in the doorway. Granted, it was quite a spectacular body, lean and hard and deliciously hung. It was annoying nonetheless. "And just like Lorin, too," I thought.

It wasn't until I had thought this last that the full shock hit home. It's bad enough to have a perfectly sedate and proper get together spoiled by the entrance of a naked male who insists on playing with himself in full view of the other guests. But when that naked dick-fondling male happens to be someone that you know beyond question has been dead for five years—that, I think, is more than any host should be expected to take in his stride.

About his death there was no question, either. I had watched them lower that same pretty body, although not in quite the same condition, into the ground.

"Paul, what on earth...?" Margo exclaimed with good reason. At the moment of Lorin's entrance, I had been in the act of refilling her cocktail glass. In the moment or so since, I had continued to pour unceasingly, with the result that what the glass could not accommodate was now overflowing into Margot's lap.

"Oh, I am sorry," I cried. I righted the pitcher, but not before the front of her dress had been thoroughly soaked. She jumped up, not quite gracefully and held her skirt out in front of her.

"I should think you are sorry," she said. "What in Heaven's name were you thinking of?" She made fluttering little attempts to wipe away the excess with a lacy handkerchief, without much success.

"Thinking of?" I stooped down to lend a hand and my own handkerchief. I should have thought the reason for my consternation would be obvious to anyone in the room. "Why, I was looking at...."

Fortunately, I looked up just then, to find the doorway empty. My eyes swept the room. All of the guests were properly trousered and skirted. Lorin was nowhere among them.

"Well, of course he couldn't be," I said aloud, looking back at the doorway. A dead man, after all, could not be attending a cocktail party in any state of dress—or undress, as the case might be.

"Who couldn't be?" Margo asked, bringing me back to the present moment. I looked up to find her staring at me with an expression of bewilderment, which no doubt was entirely justified.

"Oh, nothing," I said, busying myself with making the stain on her dress worse than it had been to begin with. Whatever had caused my weird mirage—and that was all it could have been—I certainly was not going to make a complete fool of myself by telling anyone else about it. I had a notion as to how this group would react if I told them about seeing a naked dead man in the doorway, shaking his cock at me in a lewd manner.

"Paul, are you all right?" Margo asked.

"Well, of course I'm all right," I said. I gave up on the stain as a bad job and stood. I had set the cocktail pitcher on the table beside us, and I retrieved it now and started to fill my own glass. "Just because I happened to spill a drink," I began—and there he was again, this time leaning against the back of a chair just beyond Margo, his now stiff rod pointed at the back of her head for all the world as though he meant to shoot into her wispy coiffure.

I don't know what my expression must have been. For a moment I was struck dumb. I stayed that way until Margo fairly squealed, "Paul!"

I blinked and looked at her, to discover that I had managed to pour the rest of the martinis down the front of her dress. By this time, she was actually dripping on the carpet.

"Oh, God," I said. I put the pitcher down on the side table with such unwarranted force that it shattered. Ice cubes and splinters of glass went flying in all directions. "Here, let me...."

"No, never mind." She brushed me away with a nervous laugh. "I think I had better go upstairs and try to repair the damage as best I can. It's a Givenchy, too. Darling, are you sure...how many drinks have you had, anyway? I haven't been watching."

"Only a couple," I mumbled, but in fact I was not really paying her much attention. I was looking around the room, stupidly. Of course he was gone again. He had disappeared the moment Margo shouted.

I rubbed my hand over my forehead. I didn't feel as though I had a fever, and I certainly had not been drinking *that much*. However much it took to create that sort of hallucination, I was sure I hadn't had it. I made a mental note to talk to my doctor about this. Somehow the idea of having hallucinations of any sort didn't sound healthy, notwithstanding that I had been feeling perfectly healthy of late. Something had to be wrong. Normal people just didn't see these things—or, if they did, they had to a man neglected to tell me about it.

"Maybe I'd better take an aspirin," I decided aloud. By this time, needless to say, I had made myself the object of some very puzzled stares.

"Look, maybe it's time we should be clearing out of here," one of the men said, laying a most solicitous hand on my shoulder.

Far from being grateful for the gesture, I was annoyed at being treated as though I were in my cups. Whatever was wrong with me, it was not a result of drinking. I still felt in control of my senses, or reasonably so, at least.

"Don't be silly," I told him. "Why don't you all just go ahead and enjoy yourselves? You know where the liquor is. Give me five minutes to get some pills working and I'll be back in full gear, all right?"

With my best air of nonchalance, I nodded around the room and made my way to the stairs. It was a relief to have a minute to myself to try to collect my scattered thoughts. In the bathroom, I shook two aspirin into my hand, swallowed them, and followed them down with a chaser of cold water. After that, I went into my bedroom and lay across the bed, letting my head hang down over the edge. Someone had told me once that it was good for the circulation. What they had not told me was that poor circulation would produce visions—lewd visions, at that.

Lorin Gebhard. The name echoed in my consciousness. What on earth had brought him to my mind, tonight of all nights? Not, of course, that he wasn't entitled to some place there, if I was to be perfectly fair. After all, he had once fully occupied all of my thoughts and emotions—but that had been five years ago, and during those years he had been gradually but firmly relegated to one of those dim corners that one only peeks into occasionally.

Why on earth had he come bounding out of that corner tonight, and into the middle of my cocktail party?

"Well, there's a perfectly logical reason for it, now that I give it some thought," I told myself, closing my eyes for a moment. For one thing, I was only a few weeks away from my marriage to Margo. It probably wasn't too surprising that that should bring to mind my other "marriage," to Lorin, even if I had never heard of a similar case.

8

I had to smile at the word "marriage." Even in the homosexual sense, marriage didn't quite seem to describe the relationship we'd had. It was more like a roller coaster ride, a flight with Dorothy in a cyclone, an acid trip—and then had come the shock of his death. How ironic that Lorin, who had always boasted that he had never found anything so big that he couldn't get it down his throat, should have choked to death on something so small as a diamond, and one from his own cufflink at that, which had accidentally fallen into his drink. I always thought he would have been pleased to know what an expensive instrument Fate had chosen for his death. He had never done anything in an ordinary fashion.

There had been the predictable shock, of course, and a large measure of grief, but in all honesty, over a period of time, I had become gradually aware of another feeling: a sense of relief.

Lorin had been wild and wonderful, and I had been crazy about him. He could be fun, witty, entertaining. He was a magnificent sex partner—handsome, well hung, truly uninhibited. The truth was, however, he had been just too much for any one man—probably too much for a dozen men. God knows, he'd had more than a dozen while he had been with me. For every wonderful gesture, there had been a score of disastrous or horrifying acts that had made my hair stand on end, and turned some of it gray in the process. For every moment that I had loved him, there had been hours when I'd gladly have shoved that fatal diamond down his throat myself. I didn't really regret any of the months we had been together, but eventually, and only when I was by myself, I had to admit the simple fact that I wasn't altogether sorry it was in the past.

It *was* in the past, too. That was the important thing just now. It was irrevocably in the past. Lorin was dead, and he certainly could not have been tripping around the party downstairs in the altogether, although it was the sort of stunt he'd have been likely to pull when he was alive. I had merely experienced some sort of hallucination, probably brought about by the lobster Newburg the night before, which had always done a number on my tummy. Now that I called it to mind, I even thought at the time it had tasted a bit strange.

I felt a light hand at my temples. Margo apparently had slipped quietly into the room to see how I was feeling. I sighed and reached for her hand. Dull though she sometimes was, she was thoughtful.

"I'm all right now, darling," I assured her gratefully.

"I'm so glad. You looked just dreadful downstairs."

The voice was not Margo's. It was every bit as masculine as the hand I had clasped. I felt a shiver zigzag its way up my spine. I didn't have to open my eyes to identify the voice or the hand. The truth was, I didn't even much want to open my eyes at all. They more or less opened of their own accord.

It was he, of course. He smiled as my eyes opened, and winked, just the way he had always greeted me before. "Hello, darling," he said, leaning over to kiss me.

I ducked. This was carrying indigestion a bit too far, to my way of thinking, and I was not about to start necking with undigested Lobster Newburg.

"Now, wait a minute," I stammered, managing to get to my feet on the opposite side of the bed. "Stay away from me, you…you…." I couldn't, in my consternation, decide just what to call him. I didn't want to be tactless, after all.

"Tiger," he supplied with a mischievous grin. Fortunately he did not try to follow me to my side of the bed. At least, he hadn't yet.

"Tiger?"

"That's what you used to call me. Don't tell me you've forgotten."

"I haven't forgotten. But you aren't you." I paused for a second or two to stare at him. Blond hair. Flashing blue eyes. Large endowment, soft now but still impressive. He certainly looked like him. "Are you?" I added faintly.

"Well, of course, who else?" he said.

"You can't be," I said, shaking my head stubbornly. "You're gone."

"How can I be gone when I'm here?" he asked.

"What I mean is, you…." But I still couldn't think of a nice way to put it.

"Crossed over," he suggested. "That's the term we like to use with one another. No one wants to be called dead, not

10

to his face, anyway. It has an unpleasant ring to it, don't you think?"

It sounded reasonable, all right, but then, I had never before talked to anybody who was really dead, in the literal sense.

"Well, what are you doing crossing back?" I asked. "I didn't think that was allowed."

He got up off the bed, but still on the other side. For an hallucination, he was certainly authentic. Standing, moving, every detail, every gesture was Lorin. He turned slightly and there was that funny little dimple at the small of his back, just above his cheeks, that I had loved to kiss on my way down.

"Sometimes it is," he said, looking around the room. "Don't you have any cigarettes?"

"Do you smoke?" I asked. I found it hard to imagine a mirage puffing on a cigarette. That seemed to credit lobster Newburg with quite a bit.

He shrugged. "I don't know," he said. "I was just going to find out. This is my first trip, you know, and it's been so long since I had a cigarette."

"I left mine downstairs," I said. "Look, why don't you just make yourself comfortable and I'll run down and get them." I edged toward the door, contemplating the possibilities of escape, at least for a moment.

"Oh, don't bother," he said. "There'll be plenty of time to try that later."

I came to a halt. "Later? Do you mean you plan to stay around for a while?"

He cocked an eyebrow. "Well, don't look so dismayed at the prospect, love. I can remember when you wanted nothing so much as to have me with you."

"That was before," I reminded him.

"Have things changed so much?" he asked, starting around the bed toward me.

"Don't touch me," I ordered, shrinking back against the wall.

"Don't be a goose. I feel just exactly like I always did. Which, if you'll recall, was rather nice. See?" He put out a hand and touched my cheek very lightly with one finger. I

11

had to admit that it didn't feel at all ghostly. At least, it was not what I would have expected "ghostly" to feel like.

"You feel, well, real," I said hesitantly.

"Of course," he said. "But I don't always. Look." He waved his hand right through my arm without my feeling a thing. This was much more what one expected a ghost to be. I had a violent case of goose pimples.

"If you have any sort of control over that," I said, "I think I would just as soon you stayed solid. It's less disquieting, you understand."

"No problem," he said. "The hard part, actually, is staying visible. It's easier with you because of our, shall we say, closeness. A matter of rapport, in a manner of speaking. That's why you saw me downstairs but nobody else could. They weren't on my wavelength. That's putting it rather crudely, but you'd never understand the terms we use."

"You mean no one but me can see you?" This was at least some comfort.

"Not unless I really work at it. Probably in time I'll get better at it. That's what others have told me who have made the trip. But it takes a lot of concentration, and just now I don't think I could manage it for more than a short time."

"Please, don't manage it on my account," I said quickly. "I'm confused enough in my own mind without having to explain to everyone else downstairs what you're doing here. Which brings me back to the point. How did you manage to come back? And why?"

"Well, the *how* was a bit sticky. I'd applied for a pass a long time ago, just to come back and visit you, but there is so much red tape involved. You can't imagine. It just goes on forever. Then, when I heard about this marriage of yours, to that creature…"

"You mean Margo?"

"Who else are you marrying, pray tell, Moby Dick?"

"How on earth did you heart about it, anyway?" I asked. "I shouldn't have thought you got newspapers over there."

He grinned and wagged a finger at me. "Now you're getting confused with your terminology. It wasn't on earth, you see. But if you must know, it was Walter King. He brought all the details with him."

12

"Oh, that's right," I said, remembering. "Walter did die—excuse me, pass over recently."

"How did he go, by the way? He's been giving us the most elaborate tales about a Texas oil millionaire and a speeding Rolls Royce, which no one believes for a minute. I promised some of the girls I'd get the—pardon the expression—straight story while I was here."

I couldn't help smiling. Gossip, it seemed, was immortal, especially among queens. "I'm afraid it wasn't anything nearly so glamorous," I said, glad for the chance to get back at Walter King, who had knifed me plenty of times—rest his soul. "It seems there had been a prowler in his neighborhood who was inclined to molest the ladies while he robbed them. So, Walter said that if people were being molested, he was going to leave his back door wide open and a sign up to show where it was."

"I shouldn't have thought a sign was necessary," Lorin said, "The people who have been through that one's back door. God knows, if he had ever shown it to me, I'd probably have crossed over a year sooner from the shock."

"At any rate," I said, "He left the door open, and they found him the next day, stone cold but smiling from ear to ear. Do you know, they never could get that grin off his face. It gave an odd impression at the funeral. They caught the man, by the way. He said it was an accident."

"Going to bed with Walter would be. But I hope they hang him. He sounds like someone we could use over where I am. All those goody-two-shoes."

I smiled. Then I remembered. "You've gotten me off the subject again, damn it. We were talking about why you came back."

"But I explained that. When I heard about this farce of a marriage, I figured I was needed in a hurry, so I just came anyway, without waiting for all that red tape."

"Then you're sort of AWOL?"

"Not quite." Lorin cocked his head to one side. I recognized that gesture. He had always used it when he was about to excuse his actions. "Actually, I borrowed a pass from another guy. He wasn't too awfully keen on using it himself, and he had taken sort of a shine to me, so we worked out a little trade, to use an appropriate phrase."

I said, dryly, "Still using the same old worm for bait, I see."

"Don't be insulting. I don't think worm is a very appropriate word."

"Whatever word you use, it's still hustling. And you're wasting your efforts anyway. I don't see what my marriage has to do with you."

"It's preposterous, that's what it has to do with me," he said. "In the first place, you could think of my social standing. Everyone is giggling and saying it's because I was a drab that you're giving up the normal life and marrying a woman. Besides, I can't be expected just to sit around and watch you do anything so silly."

"You're a fine one to talk about doing silly things," I said. I was pouting, of course. He had always managed to make me do that. Even when I was utterly in the right, he could twist things around to make it seem that I was the one being unreasonable. I particularly resented it under the present circumstances.

"Besides," I said, "I like women. You know that. And I need someone like Margo. She's very sweet, and lovely, and she's stable. That's more than you ever were, I might add."

"Oh, stable!" Lorin threw his hands into the air. "There's something about that word that calls to mind horse shit and other odious matters." He plopped down heavily on the bed and gave me a shrewd look. "And don't give me this noble I-like-women routine. I haven't missed very much, you know. Margo Sellers, isn't that her name? And the name of that engineering firm you work for?"

I frowned and tried to look indignant. "Sellers and Sellers," I admitted. "But if you think...."

"How are you doing with them, anyway?" he interrupted me rudely. "When I left, you were on just about the lowest rung of the ladder."

"Well, I've done a little better," I said.

"A little?"

"I'm head of the planning department. But that's got nothing to do with Margo. It's just possible I might have some ability. Give me a little credit, for Christ's sake."

"Oh, I do, darling, I do. And aren't you looking forward to another little promotion ere long?"

It was very annoying to argue with someone who apparently knew every little thing that was going on in my life. It seemed to me a man ought to be entitled to keep some secrets, particularly from someone who is dead.

"Since you already seem to know everything, yes, there's been some talk, but nothing definite, of course, but some hints of my maybe becoming a full partner in the firm."

"After the honeymoon, right?" Lorin smirked.

"Now cut that out! It's just possible, you know, that I could be marrying Margo because I'm in love with her. It's just possible."

Lorin threw his head back and laughed. "Oh, I guess it is possible, but it does boggle the mind, darling, I must say."

"Well, so do you," I said angrily, "If I must be blunt. I've a good mind…."

"Paul?" It was Margo's voice, from the hall.

"I do believe it's Minnie the Mermaid," Lorin said in a lower voice.

Before I could think what to do, Margo had reached the door, opened it, and swept into the room. I looked at her in dismay and then back to the bed. Thank Heaven he had had the tact to leave—or at any rate, he couldn't be seen. I let out the breath I had been holding and turned back to Margo.

"Are you feeling better," she asked.

"Oh, yes, much," I said.

"I don't know." She gave me a funny look. "You look as though you had seen a ghost."

*THE GAY HAUNT*, BY VICTOR J. BANIS

# CHAPTER TWO

I must confess that I wasn't sorry to see the party guests leave. Margo and I stood at the front door to see them out. They each thanked us insincerely for a lovely time, and with equal insincerity we thanked them for coming. At last, with a great sigh of relief, I closed the door soundly after the last of them.

"Thank Heavens, that's over," Margo declared, returning to the living room, which was a shambles. "I must say it was certainly a unique afternoon."

"I'll drink to that." I poured myself a stiff shot of gin, added a drop of vermouth and gulped it down.

"Are you sure you should?" she asked, giving me a long hard look.

"Oh, for Pete's sake, Margo," I snapped, "I've told you a dozen times, I'm nowhere near being loaded."

"You don't usually go around pouring drinks on me," she countered.

"I'm sorry about that." A nasty stain on the skirt of her expensive dress served as a reminder of my clumsiness. "But it wasn't a result of drinking. I'm just nervous, that's all."

"About what?"

"A man has a right to be nervous when he's about to get married, hasn't he?"

She softened slightly at that. "Oh, you men. I suppose we shouldn't be quarreling, but you *have* been acting a bit strange, though. Darling, are you sure something isn't bothering you?"

"What could be bothering me?" I put an arm about her and pulled her closer to kiss the tip of her nose lightly. What

17

I most wanted was to close the conversation before the wrong thing was said.

"I don't know," she said. "What sort of thing does bother a man when he decides to get married? Maybe there is some ghost from the past."

"Don't say that." I jerked away from her irritably and turned my back so she wouldn't see my reaction to her remark—but not fast enough.

"There is something," she said emphatically. "Paul, there's something about your past that you haven't told me, something that's come back to haunt you."

"There's no such thing," I insisted. I decided that I needed another drink and poured my glass full of gin again, foregoing the vermouth.

"And the drinking proves it. You don't normally belt them down like that."

I put the glass down sharply. She came up behind me and put her arms about me, gently leaning her cheek against my back.

"Is it some other woman?" she asked in her softest voice, a tacit promise of understanding included in her tone. "Some old girlfriend that you've seen again? I know what these things can be for a man, darling, honestly I do. Daddy told me all about that sort of thing. Tell me the truth, please, that's all I ask."

I kept my back to her and considered the possibility. Margo was my fiancée. She had a right to know the truth, but could I expect her to understand and believe it? I didn't understand or believe it myself, as a matter of fact.

"Margo," I said in a tentative voice, "Suppose I told you that, in a manner of speaking, I was *seeing* someone? I mean, well, not exactly...."

"Paul!" The shock in her voice brought me around to face her. Her eyes, soft and understanding a minute before, were wide now with astonishment and anger. All the gentleness had vanished.

"I knew it," she said. "All this time you've been whispering sweet nothings to me, and then sneaking right off somewhere to cavort with someone else, probably some

18

common tramp. How despicable of you. Oh, Paul, how could you?"

I sighed inwardly and shook my head. It was no use trusting Margo to understand, nor could I ask her to be reasonable. She did not have much reasoning ability. Of all the people to whom I could explain my problem, she was the least likely.

"Margo, my dear," I said, as reassuring as I could be, "I can truly assure you that there isn't another woman. In fact, there isn't a single human being involved in my behavior. It's just that I'm tired, that's all."

My hand went automatically to my forehead. At least that was the truth. I was tired. My mind had worn itself out trying to grasp what had happened to me, and without any success.

"Oh, you poor dear," she said solicitously, all concern again. She came to pat my shoulder. "I'm going to tell Daddy he's working you too hard. You should take tomorrow off and just rest the whole day."

"Yes, maybe that would be a good idea," I agreed. Another thought had occurred to me. So far, I was the only one who had seen Lorin, but he had indicated that he could make it possible for others to see him too, and I knew him well enough to guess that he wasn't likely to pass up too many opportunities to create excitement. What if he followed me to work in the morning? I didn't think Sellers and Sellers was ready for that.

"And I'll tell you what else," Margo said. "You're going to soak in a hot tub while I fix you a nice toddy, and then I'm going to rub your back for you and tuck you into bed like a little boy." She gave me what she considered her coquettish smile, which was in fact something of a lopsided leer.

I tried dutifully to rise to the occasion. "Hasn't anyone ever warned you about the dangers of tucking little boys into bed?"

"Um huh. You've been neglecting some things lately, you know."

"We'll have to correct that, won't we?" I said. I chucked her under the chin playfully and gave her backside a slap. "All right, off to the toddy factory with you. I'll get along with that bath you suggested. Who knows, maybe that's just what I do need."

Alone in my room, I put my clothes away neatly and took a robe with me to the bathroom. I was relieved that there had been no further sign of Lorin since he had disappeared earlier. Maybe, I thought, his pass had expired or some such thing. Or maybe I had actually dreamed it all. That was possible. I hadn't realized it before, but I did feel rather overtired. No doubt that could have caused it.

It was comforting to climb into the big tub filled with hot water and, one of my favorite luxuries, big mountains of foamy, citrus scented bubbles. I sank down into the depths, letting myself relax.

Yes, that was it. I had fallen asleep on the bed, and all the rest had been a dream—a very realistic dream, but a dream nonetheless. Beyond doubt, that was the explanation, and Margo was right, I had been pushing myself too hard, what with the job and the impending wedding and all.

"A couple of days off," I said aloud, "And I'll feel like a new man." I splashed the water playfully with one hand. To my consternation, it splashed back.

"How marvelous, who's he going to be?" Lorin appeared as he spoke, grinning widely at me from the opposite end of the tub.

"Now this is ridiculous," I sputtered, clutching a handful of bubbles before me. "It's bad enough when you appear without invitation in my bedroom, but I'll not have you popping into my tub with me."

"Paul, darling, don't you remember the things we used to do in the tub? And what about the showers, hmm?" He winked smugly. "You all the time coming in to wash my back, inside and out. Honestly, with all that soap and your goings-on, I stayed clean clear through."

"Quit that," I said, jerking my foot away from his tickling finger. "And I don't want to hear any more of your dirty stories. You were the one who was always dropping the soap, as I recall."

"Oh, you do remember," he exclaimed. "It's going to be such fun, isn't it, rediscovering all these things." He got up

20

on his knees and came towards me, floating, as it were, on top of the bubbles.

"That's it," I snapped, scrambling up and out of the water before he got to me. "That is just exactly it. Now, I am not going to put up with this, I tell you." Still dripping water and lemon bubbles, I threw open the door to my bedroom. "Out," I shouted. "Get out!"

"What on earth for?" Margo asked. She stood just inside my bedroom, bearing a steaming mug on a tray.

Of course, he had disappeared immediately. I couldn't even tell if he were still in the tub until I heard him blowing bubbles from under the water.

"I wasn't talking to you," I apologized lamely to Margo. "I mean, I wasn't talking to anyone exactly. You see, there was...a fly. Yes, that's it, a fly in the bathroom, and it kept buzzing me and buzzing me and flying around my head, don't you see? So I finally yelled at it, 'out, get out.' Except I didn't know you were out here when I said it."

"Oh." She looked unconvinced and peered uncertainly around me to assure herself that the bathroom really was empty. There was a loud noise from the tub, closely approximating the breaking of wind.

"Excuse me," I said quickly.

She gave me another odd look. "Maybe you had better put a robe on," she said, "You're dripping."

"Yes, yes, I will," I said, grateful for something I could cope with, and to have Margo safely out of the bathroom. I joined her in the bedroom in my robe. She was seated on the far side of the bed. My toddy was waiting on the nightstand. I took a sip of it. Margo made what was unquestionably the world's worst toddy, but I wasn't particularly interested in the drink just then. Another idea had occurred to me.

There was one thing I could do to convince Lorin that I was sincere in my interest in Margo and in going straight; and, incidentally, to discourage any interference on his part. I put the drink aside and leaned back on the bed, reaching for Margo.

"It's about those things I've been neglecting," I said, pulling her to me.

"You ought to drink your drink while it's hot," she suggested, but without offering any resistance.

"There are other things hotter," I whispered luridly. I glanced over her shoulder to see if we had an audience, but if so he was remaining invisible.

"My, you are feeling better," she said when I kissed her. I had decided to make the show a good one.

"You always feel divine," I said, running a hand over her plump bottom. "I think I'll turn out the light while you get more comfortable." I knew from past experience that Margo preferred to make love in the dark. I didn't mind. She was very nice, but she wasn't a terribly pretty girl.

The truth was, although I wouldn't have told Lorin so, I didn't find sex with women as wild and sensational as other men seemed to. Not that I didn't enjoy a good romp. I had made up my mind that I was heterosexual in that respect, but I couldn't honestly say balling Margo drove me wild. I suppose I had Lorin to thank for that too. Whatever faults he might have had, and they were legion, sex had always been his best asset. Sucking, fucking, rimming, shrimping—whatever turned you on. He did it all, and did all of it better than anybody else.

All the same, on this occasion I was determined that sex with Margo would be great, just in case anyone was watching and needed convincing. I approached the session with such determination that I found myself more than ordinarily aroused. While we kissed, my hands explored the softness of her naked body. I squeezed her breasts and felt the nipples harden against my fingers. I ran a hand over her belly and down, trailing my fingers through the thick hair below, caressing the lips, tentatively slipping a finger into the warm, moist interior.

Margo ran the fingers of her hand through my hair. The other hand clutched at my shoulders, while the remaining hand, with a boldness unusual for her, reached down to grope and fondle my stiff rod.

It hit me after a moment: one, two, three hands. I felt for her left shoulder, followed that arm to the hand at my hair. I followed the right arm to the hand at my shoulder. That left the hand that was now jerking me attached to neither of her shoulders.

"Now cut that out," I sputtered, sitting up suddenly. I reached for the light and snapped it on furiously. Of course there was no one to be seen, but the hand was still to be felt, moving stubbornly up and down. I shoved at it hard, trying to get it away from me.

"Now what? Have you gone crazy?" Margo asked in bewilderment, staring at me with wide eyes. She was rubbing one breast where I had unceremoniously poked her with an elbow.

"I had a cramp," I said, managing at last to get my cock away from him. I rubbed my thigh in the way of a demonstration. "It's all right now."

"Well, turn out that light, then," she said. She reached for the sheet and pulled it up modestly over her naked body.

"No," I said, glancing around uneasily. Somehow I felt safer with the light on.

She pouted and pulled the sheet up higher, looking me up and down with disapproving boldness. "You know I don't like it with the lights on. You look so funny, poking out like that in front."

"Men are supposed to poke," I said. I moved back to her, putting my arms around her. There was one sure way to prevent Lorin from getting his hands on my dick: I could put it out of his reach. I set myself to coaxing Margo back into the mood.

"You certainly are acting peculiar," she repeated, but she let me tug the sheet away. I moved down and took one rosy nipple into my mouth, nibbling on it gently. In a minute I felt her legs move apart a little. I slid cautiously down between them.

"Love makes a man peculiar," I said. I wriggled my butt.

"Oh, Paul." That seemed to satisfy her, and it took only a few more minutes to restore her to readiness. A little concentrated finger work, a quick trip down in the valley, and she was hot and juicy again. I got into place and guided the knob in, making a gentle entry—Margo disliked anything rough or impetuous. With her, fucking had to be gentle and smooth, and just a little dull. I had never quite gotten used to the idea of subdued and refined sex.

I had thought that watching me having it on with Margo would discourage my invisible visitor. Far from it. On the contrary, it only seemed to give him more ideas, which he promptly decided to act upon. I had no more than gotten nicely into her before I felt an exploratory probing at my ass, and a finger began to push meaningfully against me. Lorin, it seemed, had decided to occupy himself.

Now, even if I had been inclined toward threesomes and such, and even if he had been a flesh and blood partner, this still wouldn't have been my route. I had never gone for having my ass stuffed, and he knew it. I jerked away from him, alarmed by the pressure he was exerting.

"Ouch," Margo protested beneath me, "Be careful, darling, please."

"Sorry," I said. He was still after me, and now it wasn't a finger against my hole, but the determined head of a very stiff, very large prick. Lorin had my cheeks spread and was trying hard to shove it into me. I squirmed, trying to evade his movements, and reached behind clumsily with one hand to try to push him away.

"Paul, you don't have to squirm and wriggle so much," Margo said, "And you're hurting me. You weigh a ton."

I couldn't very well explain to her that at this point she had two of us on top of her, nor could I raise up to relieve her of the weight without backing right up on to a big dick. Invisible or not, what I could feel of him just now was terribly solid, and glued hard to my hole. I felt his hot breath on my ear and heard just the faintest whisper of a laugh as that opening yielded slightly to his stubborn prodding.

That son of a bitch, I swore to myself. I pulled away again, at the same time thrusting down hard into Margo.

"Sorry," I said. "Ouch!" This time he followed me insistently, poking away at my vulnerability.

"Ouch yourself," Margo said, pushing against me. "Get up."

I tried to comply, but once again I found myself backing up to Lorin. "I can't," I told her. "Don't," I hissed over my shoulder.

"Don't?" Margo echoed me. "I certainly won't. Let me up."

She shoved hard at my shoulders. I held on to her and rolled forcefully onto my side, taking her with me. For a moment the pressure on my hole was gone, but only for a moment. Then he was there again, trying to push my legs apart with his, holding my hips steady with his hands and shoving his cock against me.

"Hold still," a voice whispered in my ear.

"I will not hold still," Margo answered for me. "Let go of me this instant."

"No, darling," I tried to argue, "Give me just a minute…."

"I think it's time you got royally fucked," Lorin declared aloud.

"Don't be crude," Margo snapped. She was still trying to squirm free and I was still trying to squirm out of Lorin's path. Neither of us was successful. I felt a searing pain as he made an especially forceful thrust and suddenly that big knob was crammed inside me. Lorin had gained his end—or mine, as it were.

"Jesus," I yelped as he drove it home. The result was that Margo was suddenly given all that I had and some I hadn't suspected I had. She let out a yelp of her own.

"I can't take that," I said aloud, at the moment too concerned with sparing the rest of my burning backside from that driving rod of his to care what Margo heard or thought.

"Well, neither can I," she cried.

"All you need," Lorin suggested, "is loosening up. You ought to get fucked by a roomful of sailors some night, one right after the other. It would do you a world of good, warm up that little hole of yours."

"Paul!" Margo was fighting me like a wildcat by this time, trying to slap and kick her way free of me. "How dare you speak to me that way?"

"Lorin," I shouted, squirming and bucking, trying to dislodge my own molester before he got any deeper. The name came out without any thought on my part.

Margo decided on desperate measures. She sank her teeth viciously into my bare shoulder. I yelled with pain and jerked violently backward, rewarding Lorin with much more than an initial entry. His cock burned a fiery trail into my aching ass.

"Heaven," Lorin hissed loudly, "Do that again. It was fabulous."

"You've completely lost your mind," Margo yelled. Her move had succeeded in freeing my hold on her, and before I could grab her again, she scrambled away from me. I tried to follow her, but Lorin was still clinging to me as tightly as he could, and with the lights on I couldn't fight him off directly without making my predicament look all the more peculiar. I twisted about frantically but there was no escaping my invader. Lorin was fucking like a wildcat, pounding the hell out of me.

"What *is* wrong with you? Margo asked. She stood with her hands on her hips and stared down angrily at me. "You look as though you had St. Vitus' dance."

"It's...it's the cramps again. I'm in pain," I explained hoarsely, which was quite true. "Back here," I added. I put my hands behind me, pretending to rub while I tried to push Lorin away, or at least prevent his giving me any more. No good. He shoved my hands away and drove it in to the hairs. I knew exactly how much hard thick cock was tearing the hell out of me; I had measured that damned ten-incher enough times in the past. Right now it felt more like twenty.

"Honestly," Margo continued, "Something's gotten into you."

Lorin giggled into my shoulder. Margo shook her head. "I'm going to get dressed and go home," she said. "Maybe by tomorrow you'll feel better."

"Yes," I agreed helplessly, still squirming. "Give me a minute and I'll walk you down." If, I thought to myself, I could still walk when Lorin got out of there.

"I don't mind telling you," she said, marching toward the bathroom, "I'm plenty sore."

"So am I," I admitted quietly as the bathroom door closed behind her. "And as for you," I said in a lowered voice, "Get the hell out of there."

He clung tightly to me, pumping in and out of me a mile a minute. I knew without being told that he was pretty close to shooting his load, but I didn't care, my ass felt like it had a red hot poker up it.

"Just a minute more," he gasped, nibbling at my ear.

Margo came back before I could get free. I froze, gritting my teeth as she began donning her clothes. I had never known anyone could fuck as hard as Lorin was fucking my ass—long strokes, short strokes, twist.

"On second thought," Margo said, tugging her dress on, "I think you'd better stay in bed. And maybe a good shot of something would help."

She looked around sharply when Lorin groaned. I grimaced. That god-damned pole of his had swollen up till it felt three times as big. I couldn't very well explain to Margo that just at that moment I *was* getting a shot of something—a generous, hot load of come that filled up what little space was left in me and threatened to overflow. I found myself wondering a little hysterically if his come would be invisible.

Finally he stopped, leaning heavily against me, and I felt him starting to shrink a little. By this time I was too dazed even to try to pull away from him.

"Seriously, Paul," Margo said, fixing her gaze on me, "You look like you've had it."

"I have," I admitted wearily.

THE GAY HAUNT, BY VICTOR J. BANIS

## CHAPTER THREE

"Now you've done it," I stated, returning to the bedroom after seeing a frosty Margo to the door.

"Yes, and it was divine," a quite visible Lorin answered with a canary-eating grin. He was stretched out on the bed, puffing in lifelike fashion on a cigarette. The cause of the lingering pain in my ass was soft now, dangling limply between his downy thighs. "Do you know, darling, I should have talked you into that five years ago. I never realized what I was missing."

"You didn't exactly talk me into it this time," I told him. "And if you'd tried it five years ago, it wouldn't have been a fucking diamond that killed you." I tossed my robe onto a chair and headed to the bathroom.

"I'm going to take a shower," I said, "And then I'm going to come back in here and go to bed. And by that time I want your ass out of here and all the way back to wherever you came from. We're through, kaput, finished. As far as I'm concerned, you can drop dead—again."

Unperturbed, he followed me right into the bathroom, straight through the door I had just so dramatically slammed after myself.

"Balls," he said, unceremoniously seating himself on the john. "And speaking of that, what are you doing for a boy friend these days? Anyone I know?"

"I don't have a boyfriend," I said, hoping he wasn't about to take a ghostly crap, a prospect I found particularly disconcerting. "Can't you get it through your ephemeral skull that I no longer make it with guys? I have no interest in guys. I have gone straight, N-O-R-M-A-L, straight."

"Baloney, S-H-I-T. You always went for a sex partner whose crotch stuck out and whose chest didn't. And don't give me that old bullshit about a horse can change its spots in the middle of the stream. I've known too damn many of them."

"That's studs you're thinking of, and I'll agree you've known too damn many of them."

"And a few horses' asses, too," he said, raising his voice over the sound of the shower. "Anyway, you were always perfectly happy in the saddle."

I poked my head out through the shower curtain. "There's another old saying," I said, "About riding dead horses."

He only smiled at that and winked. "You didn't think I was so dead when I was humping you a few minutes ago," he said.

"Go to hell," I snapped, retreating into the shower.

"I've been." He appeared at my elbow suddenly, causing me to drop the soap.

"Damn it, will you stop appearing and disappearing like that," I said. I started to bend down for the soap, thought better of it with Lorin so close at hand, and stooped down instead.

"While you're down there," he said, turning toward me and rubbing his balls. They were beauties, big globes frosted with glowing golden hairs. I looked away from them, ignoring the invitation, and stood again, starting to lather myself with the soap.

"Want me to take care of your back for you?" he asked after a minute.

"You already did."

"Oh, don't be a grump," he said. He took the soap out of my hand and began to rub my back.

He had been good at this sort of thing before, and he hadn't forgotten any of his old skill. His strong fingers not only got me clean, they artfully kneaded away the tension in the muscles there.

For a moment, it seemed as though we really had stepped back in time. I found myself thinking back, despite my wish not to. Yes, he had always been impossible, and

30

maddening, but there had been good things, too. I'd be lying if I tried to deny that. The coaxing movements of his hands and the soothing spray of warm water dissipated some of my anger.

"Nice?" he asked.

"Um hmmm," I murmured, sighing deeply.

He finished splashing the soap away and turned off the water. "Come on," he said.

I followed him out of the shower and he began to dry my body with a big towel, just as he had done in the past whenever he really wanted to pamper me.

I realized suddenly that I was staring into the big mirror that covered one wall, looking at our reflections as though they were two strangers. I was taller than he, but he was somewhat stockier, and the five years since I had last seen us like this had taken their toll on me. I was softer looking, a result of not keeping up with exercises and diets. I was still good looking, I thought, even manly. I didn't have his ten inches, but eight nice thick ones were nothing to sneer at, and I had no gut, yet. But, there was a warning softness about the middle, and my hair had gone grayer, much too gray for a man in his early thirties.

Lorin, though, still looked the twenty-two he had been when he died. The sort of life he led then should have made a wreck of him, except that he was much too careful for that. Every night of carousing had been carefully balanced with an entire day in bed. Every care had been taken to keep that perfectly sculptured body solid, his skin soft and smooth, his golden hair in perfect condition. Even that dangling dong of his had been treated to moisture cream twice a day, just to keep it silky to the touch.

I looked up, into the reflection's flashing eyes, and found them looking back at me—not laughing, exactly, but gleaming with a light I remembered only too well. It was the expression I had loved best, when he had ceased being the madcap, or when he'd gotten over some temper tantrum, and wanted to make up—or when he realized he had pushed me a little too far and wanted to make sure of getting back in my good graces while he could.

31

"Am I still pretty?" he asked softly. He was still toweling me gently although I was long since dry. And I didn't need a mirror to tell me that my dick had started stretching out and upward, reaching for its full length. My balls suddenly felt all tingly. Lately the sex in my life had been routine. I hadn't even realized what was missing. It was a shock now to feel again, after an absence, a real itch to fuck.

I nodded despite myself. "Yes, very pretty," I admitted, unable to deny the fact. Hell, how could I have denied it? A stiff prick would have made a liar out of me. I sure as hell had one by this time.

"You loved me once, you know," he said. 'And I loved you, in my own funny little way. Oh, I admit there were always others. Tricks. Studs. One night stands. Quick little blow jobs. I never denied any of them, you've got to give me credit for that. But I wasn't putting you on when I told you that none of them were like you. You were the only who could make me feel truly alive, Paul. You still do, can't you tell?"

"Except there's a hell of a difference now," I said ruefully. "Then it was only a figure of speech, but now, you're not...not real."

"I'm here," he breathed, moving closer to me, so close that I seemed to feel his body heat warming me. Something brushed my leg and I looked down to see that the little devil had a stiff on again, that big, beautiful rod of his standing straight out and looking like it wanted to reach me. "What's real?" he asked softly. "I look the same. I feel the same, don't I?"

"Yes." My arms lifted around him, pulling him into my embrace. Our cocks met, greeted each other like long lost friends. His skin had the same feel of porcelain smoothness that I remembered so painfully well. I could taste the sweetness of his mouth even before it met mine—then I was kissing him and he was kissing me back, and we were straining against one another, his heat threatening to scorch me.

It was insane, utterly crazy. I knew that he was gone, that he didn't exist anymore, and yet, here he was in my arms, kissing me—and I wanted him, wanted him with all the intensity of passion that had ruled me in the past and made me a slave to his whims.

"Let's go to bed," he whispered against my cheek.

Wordlessly I went with him back to the bedroom. I reached automatically for the light switch, the way I was accustomed to doing with Margo, but he caught my hand in his.

"Leave it on," he said. "You used to like it with the lights on. You always liked to see everything."

It was true. I had always preferred that, before Margo and her stupid prudishness that insisted upon darkness—as if the body, the sexual act, were something to be ashamed of.

"Did you know, you can see the bed in that mirror there?" he asked, pointing to the mirror over the dresser. I had forgotten that too. It had been a long time since I'd had the kind of abandoned uninhibited sex that Lorin and I once shared. My blood was racing in my veins as memories flooded back to me, refusing now to be held in check. I kissed him hotly and together we sank to the bed.

Whatever magic he was using on me, it was powerful stuff. I looked up once at the mirror and saw us lying together, our bodies intertwined. In that moment, I think I'd gladly have gone to hell with him.

I pushed him back, kneeling over him, and my mouth began a journey into its past, a journey that took it downward over his heaving chest with its flat nipples that had always been sensitive, like a girl's. Across the rippling surface of his abdomen, still flat and hard, down to the cloud of gold at his crotch. His prick stood proudly erect, a bead of moisture gleaming at its tip. My eager tongue drank away the droplet, traced a path about the deep red crown, playing upon the sensitive underside. I went down, my lips gliding along the thick shaft, to his heavy balls, sucking first one and then the other into my mouth. Then, back, all the way to the gleaming cockhead.

Lorin gripped my head in his hands, guiding me, until my lips were parted by the entry of his cock. He was in my mouth, fucking back into my throat, and I was sucking a cock like no other I had ever tasted.

"Oh, Paul, Paul, it's all there," he gasped, his whole body shaking with excitement. "It's all there, all the music and the fireworks and the champagne popping, just like it always was with us!"

It was, too, only better. I didn't remember the taste of his cock so sweet, the hard flesh so silky, the scent so warm and puppyish. My hands went beneath him to the down-covered cheeks of his ass that were so firm and yet so soft. I explored the valley between them, finding the inviting softness of the entryway.

"You were the one who used to like it that way," I reminded him, taking my mouth from his cock for a moment.

"I think I still do," he said, laughing faintly. "Anyway, I think I owe you one, if you want it."

The question was rhetorical. I was burning with desire to invade that clinging softness. My joint was fairly aching for him. I lifted his legs about me, kneeling between them, and spat on my hand. I smeared saliva over my cockhead, and guided it eagerly to the pink opening he had turned up to me.

There was nothing passive about the way Lorin took a dick. There never had been. It was as if the muscles of his ass reached out and sucked you in. I thrust, pushing deep within him, surprised as I always had been at the virgin tightness. He seemed to be milking the head with muscles that nobody else even had. My chest ached with the labor of breathing. Beneath me he gasped with combined pain and pleasure.

"Oh, yes, yes," he moaned, his head rolling from side to side. He lifted his ass up to meet each thrust, our bodies slapping together, my nuts playing a tattoo on his cheeks. I was giving him all of it with each thrust and stroke, ramming everything I had into him without mercy, feeling it welcomed hotly by that clinging chamber, reveling in the reluctance with which it let me withdraw.

It couldn't last long. There was too much assaulting me—physical, mental, emotional. I felt the pressure within me building, rushing downward to the place where our bodies were joined. My ears were filled with roaring, my prick throbbed and pulsed—and my senses seemed to abandon me altogether. There was only the lunging and thrashing of our bodies and the white-hot flames within me as my climax grew and grew.

"Paul, Paul," he gasped, his hands clawing at my shoulders, "Hurry, I can't hold off for long!"

He didn't have to. It broke at last, a tidal wave of relief erupting within me, sweeping through me, down, down, and then it was shooting out of me, a torrent, filling him up.

"Paul, I'm going….going…." he managed to cry aloud.

Gone! The sensations that consumed me seemed to sweep us into another world. With me, it was figurative. With him, it was literal. I came, and he went. There was suddenly nothing beneath me but the pillow and a puddle of jism that should have been within my partner.

My hair stood on end. Memory or no memory, there was nothing the slightest bit romantic about having your partner disappear from beneath you at the exact moment you are shooting a load. From somewhere above me, he laughed.

"That wasn't funny, goddammit," I roared, rolling over and looking around for him. "What's the big fucking idea?"

"I couldn't help it," he sputtered through his laughter. "I told you, it takes practice to remain all together in solid form, practice and concentration. I haven't fully mastered it yet, for one thing, and for another, I was so busy with what we were doing, I forgot all about concentrating."

"Well, stop that damn laughing and come back down here where I can see you," I said. My dignity was hurt. For that matter, so were my balls. I had landed on them when he disappeared from beneath me, and had almost literally cracked my nuts.

"I can't, darling," he said. "Really and truly. It's like, well, my batteries are run down, that's the best way to explain it. I've got to rest until they're charged up again."

"Well, of all the…." I sat up and reached for a cigarette from the nightstand. "We never stopped with just once in the old days," I reminded him. "The first time used to be just a warm up session."

"I know." He stopped laughing and grew serious. "But I'll get better. I promise."

After a pause, he said, "Paul?"

"What?" I puffed furiously on the cigarette. It was a pain in the ass to have something brought back to you like that, something really great, and then to have it yanked away right form under your nose, so to speak.

"You're still the best, in heaven or earth," he said. "And I should know."

I grunted, trying not to show that he could still flatter me out of a bad temper. "Go get your batteries charged," I said gruffly, stubbing out the cigarette. I reached for the light and plunged the room into darkness, dropping heavily against the pillow.

"Hey," I said after a moment.

"What?" His voice was fainter and very faraway sounding by this time.

"Did you come?"

He laughed softly, a silvery sound that rang on my ears like a forgotten melody. "To hell and back," he answered.

I smiled into the darkness. It was the term he had used in the past when it had been an especially good one for him. Knowing Lorin, he had probably used the same expression with dozens of others, but at least I had the distinction of being the only one who had ever literally done just that to him.

Assuming, of course, that he did come back.

# CHAPTER FOUR

I awoke to a stream of golden California sunshine and the delicious aroma of fresh coffee. I closed my eyes again for a moment and stretched contentedly. I'd had a beautiful night's sleep, better than I had slept in months. For a moment I didn't remember why.

It came back to me then, all of a sudden: the party last night, Lorin's appearance, that ridiculous scene with Margo—and that incredibly wild sex from out of the past....

I sat upright, blinking my eyes against the morning light that fell in dusty shafts from the window. Lorin. My Lorin. He had come back from the grave.

Or had he? Had I dreamed it all, or just had too much to drink, as Margo had hinted? I shook my head experimentally—no morning after headache—and stared around the room. On the nightstand was a large mug of steaming coffee, and beside it a glass of orange juice in a nest of ice.

No one in the world but Lorin had ever awakened me that way. So far as I knew, Margo had never mastered the recipe for orange juice, let alone coffee. And at any rate, I distinctly remembered seeing her to the door the night before, unless she had made an early morning call. That hardly sounded like Margo. Anyway, the room was empty.

As if reading the questions in my mind, Lorin popped into sight at the foot of the bed. He was just as he had been the night before, bare ass naked, and I wondered fleetingly about the weather where he had been, and if ghosts were likely to catch chills. I nearly made a remark about his catching his death of cold, reconsidered it, and decided to shelve it instead. I made a mental note of it, however, in case I needed a comeback sometimes in the future. In any case, he seemed to have come from a warm climate. Remembering the way Lorin had lived, it wasn't too surprising that he had been sent where it was warm.

"Good morning, darling," he greeted me cheerfully. "You're looking terribly bright-eyed and bushy-tailed this morning. I hope you slept well."

"Then it's true," I said, reaching automatically for my morning cigarette. "You did come back. I didn't dream all that."

"I thought we went all through that last night," he said. To my consternation, my cigarette lit itself before I could get a match going. There was a tiny puff of smoke, and the end began to glow all on its own.

"Sorry," he said, seeing the look of dismay on my face. "I was just showing off a little. I thought you might get a bang out of seeing some of the tricks I can do now. I have quite a repertory."

"As I recall," I said dryly, "You always did more tricks than anyone else." I decided I didn't want the cigarette after all and stubbed it out in the ashtray. "And if you don't mind, I think I'd just as soon light my own cigarettes after this, in the conventional manner."

Lorin shrugged unconcernedly. "You always were distressingly conventional, but it's your matches, and your butt, so to speak. By the by, speaking of your butt...."

"It's still sore," I told him. "And so am I."

I started to drink the orange juice and paused to study it suspiciously. "Did you use any tricks to brew this, or is it for real?"

"Straight from your own spotless kitchen, squeezed the old fashioned way, with my lily-white hands," he assured me, placing one hand over his heart. "I felt deliciously domestic while I was about it. Picture of devoted housewife slaving for hubby's pleasure. Isn't life wonderful?"

"I suppose for you it must be particularly so," I said. "Greener pastures and that sort of thing." I emptied the glass before I thought of something. "I didn't have any oranges in the kitchen."

"I borrowed them," he said, "From that sweet woman who lives next door."

I looked up and down his naked figure. "I hope you didn't go to her door like that."

"Oh, she didn't see me. I kept myself invisible." He paused, and added, "At least, she didn't exactly see me, I should say."

I had an uneasy feeling. "What does that mean?" I asked. "Not exactly?"

"Well," he hesitated.

"Come on, let's hear it."

He shrugged. "Well, as they say, tell the truth and shame the devil." He giggled, and added, "That's considered profanity where I've been, and can get you in lots of trouble."

"Quit stalling."

"She didn't see me. Period," he said. "Only, well, I forgot, she could still see the oranges while I was carrying them. The poor dear, it upset her so, seeing a half dozen navels floating across her kitchen and right out the back door. I wish you could have seen her face."

I groaned aloud. "I hope she didn't follow the floating oranges over to my kitchen?"

"Not a chance. She was out cold before I even reached her back porch." He seemed rather proud of the mischief he had managed to get into, which was an attitude quite in keeping with his warped personality.

"And to imagine," I said after a moment, "When we first started going together, I used to worry about what the neighbors would think, seeing you coming and going at all hours. Now I have to worry bout their not seeing you coming or going."

I took the coffee with me to the bathroom. I had just finished shaving, after a long, soothing shower, when Lorin popped in—literally, as it were—to announce that breakfast was nearly ready.

For the moment, at least, he seemed to have laid aside his propensity for mischief. Breakfast was good, his conversation light and pleasant, his appearance enjoyable. It was easy to forget that he was a ghost, and simply relax with his enjoyable company. When Lorin set out to be charming, it was hard to resist him.

The mood lasted until the phone rang. He moved toward it, but I made it across the room first and snatched the instrument out of his reach. I was not quite ready to have him take my calls for me, since everyone knew that I lived alone these days. And anyone who was likely to recognize his voice, surely knew that he was dead. Either way, it might raise questions.

It was Margo on the phone, still sounding a little restrained. "I hope you're feeling better this morning," she said.

"I'm feeling great," I told her, trying not to smile at the smug grin that crossed Lorin's face. "But I must apologize to you. I'm afraid I was a bit out of it last night. I can't imagine what got into me."

Lorin clucked his tongue and put a hand on his cock in a lewd gesture. I tried to ignore him.

"Well, as long as everything's all right now, I guess no harm was done," she said. "But I do think you ought to rest for a day or two."

"I think I will. I was just about to call the office, as a matter of fact, and see if I couldn't have a week to myself."

"Now, don't you worry about that," she assured me. "I already talked to Daddy, and he said for you to take as long as you like."

I frowned at the receiver. Of course, there was nothing wrong with Margo's arranging that for me. Still, it was just the sort of thing that would encourage Lorin in his ridiculous suspicions.

"Darling," Margo said after a pause, "Who is Lorraine?"

I nearly choked on my coffee. "Who is who?" I asked after a minute.

"Lorraine. You called me by her name last night, during…while I was in your room."

"Oh. Not Lorraine, Lorin." My mind was racing about frantically, trying to come up with some sensible answer to give her.

"Lorin? All right, then, who is Lorin?"

"Nobody," I said. "I mean, nobody you know. In fact, nobody of any importance. Ouch." Lorin pinched my ass. "I knew a guy named Lorin once, a long time ago, just a casual acquaintance, and for some reason or other, he just happened to cross my mind last night. That's all there was to it. Ouch."

"That's rather a strange time for him to cross your mind, don't you think?"

"Lorin's rather a strange person," I said. I had to stifle another ouch. "Or he was, rather. He's dead now, you see."

"You thought I was lively enough last night," Lorin said with a smirk.

"Is someone there with you?" Margo asked.

"Not a living soul," I promised her, giving Lorin a warning look.

"I could have sworn I heard someone talking."

"Just the radio. Look, darling, my bacon's burning to a crisp. How about if I check with you later about dinner, okay?"

"All right," she said, sounding unconvinced. "But do promise me you will get some rest. I'm worried about you, I really am."

"My bacon's burning," Lorin said in a falsetto when I had hung up. "My ass is burning, if you want to know. I suppose that was the lascivious prune. You know, her problem is that she can't decide whether she wants to be a virgin or a whore, and she ends up a flop either way."

"I shouldn't have to remind you that she is my fiancée," I replied coolly.

"I'm afraid you do have to remind me. It's still just too much for me to remember. And you still haven't come up with a reasonable explanation, by the way. Surely a job can't mean that much to you, can it?"

"You're the one who brought my job into this. You seem determined to ignore what I've been telling you since you got here, that I'm really quite fond of the lady in question."

Lorin rolled his eyes heavenward in a gesture of despair. I found it disconcerting under the circumstances.

"There," he said, "That's just what I mean. You're fond of her. But you haven't said that you're in love with her. Look me straight in the eye and tell me that you're in love with her, if you can."

41

I tried calling his bluff, but it didn't work. As soon as our eyes met, I backed down. "Well, you always were too much of a romantic," I countered, looking away from him. "Love isn't necessarily an all-at-once thing, like in the books and the movies. In real life, people have to learn to love one another over a period of time. Sort of grow into it, as they say."

"Oh, for crap's sake," Lorin said with a derisive snort. "Did you have to learn to love me, darling? Did you and I have to grow into anything? As I recall, you went right out of your noggin the first time you laid eyes on me, and it was thoroughly mutual."

"That's different," I argued, although I was not completely clear in my own mind just why it was. "We were, well, for one thing, we were young then, or at least I was. And anyway, that wasn't love, not really. Yes," I said more emphatically, feeling that I was on safer ground now. I had been through this explanation with myself a number of times and felt quite confident with it. "That's the key thing, it wasn't actually love. It was just some sort of strange infatuation. As a matter of fact, if you looked into the subject, you would learn that two men can't really love one another, not in the true sense of the word. It takes a man and a woman, living together, sharing their joys and hardships, traveling life's highway hand in hand...."

"Good God, you've been reading your Raggedy Ann books again," Lorin interrupted rudely, ruining what I that was a pretty good line. "What bosh, what unadulterated rubbish. Maybe Minnie the Mermaid is right, maybe you had better spend a day or two in bed. You're loose in the cabanza."

"Leave Minnie—I mean, Margo—out of this," I told him. "And leave my bed out of it too."

I finished my coffee in one long gulp. I couldn't help it, I was angry all over again with his damned interference, and just when he seemed to be trying to be pleasant. What business was it of his anyway, and why should I stand here arguing my personal business with someone who did not even exist?

"I didn't ask you to come back here," I said, "And I didn't ask for your approval of my marriage. Why don't you go hang around some tombstone or rattle chains in a dusty old mansion somewhere?"

"Don't be nasty," he said in an icy voice, drawing himself up haughtily. "I will not be treated like some hobgoblin loose on Halloween."

"Halloween or not, that's exactly what you are, isn't it? Just a cheap, ordinary spook, the kind that frightens little children and gets seen by spinster ladies in their boudoirs. Only, I'm not a little children...."

"Child," he corrected me.

"...Child, and I'm not a spinster lady, and I am not at all frightened. As a matter of fact, you mean no more to me, or to anyone else, I might add, than a puff of cigarette smoke."

His eyebrows were almost to the ceiling. "Cheap, am I? Ordinary? A puff of smoke? Well, of all the...you...mortal!"

With that Lorin became, literally, a puff of smoke. Apparently he had worked himself into such a temper that he forgot to concentrate. He was gone from sight, although I heard a faint whispering noise that sounded vaguely as though he were still sputtering and fuming wherever it was he disappeared to at moments like this.

"And those tawdry stunts of yours don't impress me either," I shouted after him, not sure whether he could hear me or not. "Appearing and disappearing all the time like that. Any dead tramp could do the same thing if he wanted to— probably better, for all I know."

Luckily I was standing and not seated at the table. That unfortunate piece of furniture, still full of dishes, cups, toasters and such, tilted at a rakish angle. While I watched, one side lifted into the air and, with a sudden lurch, the table turned itself upside down. There was a terrific crash of breaking dishes, and a little stream of coffee raced by my foot.

"I see you haven't outgrown your childish tantrums, either," I said to the empty room. "For a while there, I was really beginning to think being dead for a few years had improved your disposition a little. I was almost glad to have you back, stupid as it sounds, but I see your nasty temper is no better than it ever was."

I started from the room, and paused to turn back toward the upturned table. One of the difficulties of arguing with a ghost, as I was discovering, was the problem of delivering exit lines without having any idea where to direct them, or even if they had been heard. Somehow it seemed to take the edge off slightly.

"And I'll tell you something else," I added anyway, hoping he was still within range. "There is absolutely nothing new about your present condition, not as far as I am concerned, because, Lorin, darling, you were always a little spooky."

I started for the door, and remembered something, and added, "I hope you catch your death of cold."

Apparently he was still within hearing. Half of one of the broken bowls on the floor came sailing through the air and smashed against the wall just over my head. I smiled to myself, pleased that I had been able to get his goat. Nonetheless, I walked rather more rapidly toward the front door. As I remembered, his aim always improved significantly on the second try. I picked up my keys from the hall table, grabbed a jacket from the closet, and made my escape to the outside.

Once there I remembered that I had not called the office. I wasn't going to risk going back inside, though. I decided to stop at a phone booth along the way and call. It probably wasn't necessary anyway. Margo had said that she had taken care of it for me, and it wasn't as though Mr. Sellers was going to fire me for being a little negligent or taking a few days off, not with me engaged to his daughter, and the wedding only a few weeks away.

I stopped in my tracks and frowned. There it was again, exactly the sort of thing Lorin had implied. Of course, if I were going to be one hundred percent honest with myself, these things had occurred to me before. It wasn't just that I was marrying Margo to keep my job or to improve it, but a man would be silly to overlook the obvious advantage that it gave me.

Anyone with a brain knew that people did not get ahead on their abilities alone. There were too many men with brains and real talent who never got anywhere because they were too ethical to take advantage of a situation.

Wasn't that exactly the way it had been with me? I had been with Sellers and Sellers for seven years, doing a good job, without getting a single promotion, when I met Margo. Now, just a little over a year later, I was in line for a full partnership. That certainly proved the point.

I wasn't sure, though, whether it proved my point, or Lorin's. Well, I told myself, getting ahead in my job because I fucked the boss' daughter would not mean that I didn't have genuine ability. Of course, I added, it wouldn't prove that I did have any, either.

I decided I didn't like this train of thought. This was all Lorin's doing, all this confusion in my thinking. I hadn't any questions before he had come back on the scene. Everything had been fine and crystal clear. I was not going to let him disrupt my entire life the way he had always done before. This was five years later, and I was older and wiser and no longer in love with him, as I had been previously.

My Jag was parked at the street, and as I came down the drive toward it, I caught sight of Mr. Vinson, my next door neighbor, at work on his rose bushes. He saw me at the same time, and greeted me with a gloomy, "Good morning," his round, bald head bobbing.

"Morning," I replied with as much cheer as I could muster. "How's the American Beauty this morning?"

"I take it you mean my rose bush, and not Mrs. Vinson," he said, "In which case, aphids."

"Well, then, how is the Missus?"

His head ceased to bob up and down and began to swing to and fro. He fixed sad eyes on me. "Oh, she's not well either, Mrs. Ross."

"Not aphids," I said hopefully.

"She's not well, not well at all. I've always said the woman didn't have all her marbles. Comes from her mother's side of the family, that's my guess. But I never thought she would go out completely on me."

"What seems to be the trouble?" I asked. He looked so in need of a sympathetic ear that I couldn't bring myself to pass him by without showing some concern.

"Oranges," he said.

"Oranges?" I had forgotten about the oranges. I began to get some inkling of what was coming.

"Oranges," he said again. His head went back to bobbing up and down. "Flying through the air, they was, according to her account of it. A whole pack of oranges, she says, maybe a dozen, maybe even two dozen. She says they was in the refrigerator, which is where a normal person would keep oranges, right? And she says they just up and got out of the refrigerator, like they wanted some air, you see, and then they went floating off down the street, humming to themselves. She thinks they was humming that song, *I don't stand a ghost of a chance with you.* Picture it, oranges going off to pay social calls. Humming, yet. I've got her to bed, of course, and the doc's coming around to see her later. He thinks it's her liver."

"Well, I certainly hope she's feeling better soon," I said with a guilty sensation in my stomach. I turned again toward my car, and Mr. Vinson turned back to his rose bush. Something struck me in the back of the head with a dull thud. It fell to the ground and began to roll down the driveway toward the street.

"What was that?" Mr. Vinson asked, his eyes wide and staring.

"Looks like an orange," I said, watching it roll. "A navel orange, I believe."

"An orange?" he said nervously. "Where did it come from?" He looked all around, but of course by this time there was nothing to be seen.

"Beats me," I said with the most nonchalant shrug I could manage, retreating quickly toward the car. "It just came floating through the air."

# CHAPTER FIVE

In what I took to be the safety of the car, I revved up the engine and drove hastily away, but I was mistaken in thinking Lorin could be escaped that easily. Whatever his form of locomotion, it was speedier than an XKE. I had not gone more than a block before he appeared beside me. He was still stark naked, which added somewhat to my consternation. Even in Los Angeles, driving about in broad daylight without a stitch of clothes can be a risky venture.

"Couldn't you put something on?" I demanded angrily, almost running over a gentleman who had stepped from the curb in front of me. He raised his fist, no doubt planning to swear at me, but as the low-slung car went by he had an unhindered view of Lorin's considerable physical charms. The sight left the gentleman wide-eyed and speechless, and I was spared whatever choice curse he had intended.

"This is the way we dress where I come from," Lorin replied, quite unperturbed by the reactions he was producing in other passersby. "Besides, I remember the time you said my body was so beautiful it should never be hidden by wearing clothing."

"I never said it while we were driving around town," I protested, taking the first corner that would get me off the busy boulevard onto a side street. "You could get arrested for dressing like that."

"They can't arrest a ghost," he said with a giggle. "Even if it were kosher, and I don't think the law makes any mention of us, it still would be awfully difficult to accomplish."

"Well, they could arrest me."

"But you have clothes on," he pointed out. "Besides, that's not much of an argument. You could have been arrested for literally dozens of things we used to do. Think of the times you sucked on this." He put a hand on his cock. "It was perfectly illegal every time."

"Yes, but that's different."

"How different?"

I had to think about that for a minute. "For one thing," I said, "We didn't do it driving around in a car, either."

"That's not because you didn't think of it," he said. "I happen to remember one night coming home from Santa Barbara, when I had to make you quit because I was in danger of coming and sending us sailing off into the ocean."

That memory made me chuckle despite myself. "Yeah, I had forgotten all about that," I said.

I let my thoughts fly back for a moment. It had been one of those heavenly nights that California sometimes affords—the sky as clear and lovely as a bowl by Steuben, the air, warm and balmy, ruffling our hair in the convertible. The traffic rushing by on either side had seemed to be light years away. We were both happily, pleasurably high on champagne and romance. My hand on Lorin's leg, his growing response, my silly urge to take him into my mouth, taste his sweet flesh against my tongue, oblivious to an occasional stare or a horn blast from other motorists.

I shook my head to dislodge the scene. It had become too vivid. My pants suddenly felt uncomfortably tight.

"I was younger then," I said crossly, shifting position to make my hard-on less conspicuous. "And a little giddy, I guess."

"And now you're an old man," he said with a sarcastic edge to his voice. "Five short years and you're old and stuffy and dull as shit."

"If you find my company so boring, the ideal solution would be to go back to wherever it is."

"Maybe I will," he said. He glanced in my direction and I could tell from the change of voice that he had spotted what I had been trying to hide. "My, my," he said, "Maybe I won't either."

He reached across the seat to squeeze my dick. "Quit that," I snapped, trying to push his hand away. I had been driving about on more or less deserted side streets, trying to avoid those thoroughfares where other traffic would be exposed to the hazard of Lorin's nudity, but isolation is hard to come by on the streets of Los Angeles, and I was approaching a busy intersection.

"Well, I haven't gotten old and stuffy," Lorin said. He started undoing my fly.

"Lorin," I protested. Engrossed in trying to keep my cock in my pants, I forgot about the stop sign in front of me. Suddenly I was out into the intersection. There was a blaring of horns and a squealing of tires. I swerved wildly around a taxi, jumped a center divider, and roared down the wrong side of the street at breathtaking speed.

By this time, Lorin had taken advantage of my fright to get my cock out of my pants. He was on his knees on the seat, his bare ass in the air and his head in my lap. Those determined lips of his closed over my knob while I skidded around an oncoming car. Ahead, a vegetable truck loomed large. I could imagine the view the driver was getting through my windshield: my frightened face and Lorin's pleasingly molded ass, side by side, so to speak. The truck careened in one direction while I careened in the other, back across the center island. Tomatoes splashed across the car and the street.

"Lorin," I protested, struggling to get him away from my meat, but getting Lorin off a cock once he had settled to his task was no easy feat, especially if one was trying to pilot a Jag at the same time. And my cock wasn't helping things, either, responding instinctively to his skillful ministrations. My balls were tingling, though I wasn't sure how much of my excitement was being produced by the blowjob I was getting and how much by my fear.

I had a glimpse of blue and a surprised face as we shot by a motorcycle cop. "Now you've done it," I said, glancing at the rear view mirror. There were red lights flashing in it.

"Not quite," Lorin mumbled, "But I think it's getting close."

"There's a cop after us," I said, trying harder than ever to get free, "You've got to quit."

"Like hell," he said, and with that, he disappeared. That is, he went invisible. I could still feel him, however. Not only was he still going to town on my prick, which now appeared to be standing fiercely in the air of its own accord, but he also suddenly gave my foot a shove, pressing the gas pedal to the floor. The Jag shot forward like it had been fired out of a cannon.

"Are you completely off your rocker?" I shouted, trying to get my foot up. "We can't outrun a cop."

"We will until I've finished with this," he said, taking his mouth off my dick for a minute. "You know I won't quit till it's done. Besides, I think you're almost there, aren't you?"

"How in hell would I know?" I cried. We were hitting just shy of a hundred. Ahead of us a light turned red. I hit the horn hard. Something shot along my spine. I wasn't altogether sure if I was coming or pissing in my pants, but something happened. My blood was already racing, my heart pounding, my head spinning, my skin tingling. A simple orgasm wasn't going to make much difference.

We went through the intersection to the accompaniment of horns, brakes and shouts. Lorin smacked his lips noisily and I felt cool air on my cock. Presumably he had gotten a load out of me. He let go of my foot and the speedometer needle dropped back around the dial.

I had just time to get myself tucked back into my trousers before the motorcycle cop pulled alongside and waved me to the curb. Lorin gave one contented sigh and that was the last evidence of his presence, at least for a while.

"Okay," the cop said as he walked up to my window, "Where's your buddy?"

"Buddy?" I gave an innocent look around the seemingly empty interior of the car. "I don't know who you mean."

"The one who had his balls hanging out the window," he snapped.

"You must be mistaken," I said. I had decided that my only hope lay in playing dumb.

"Don't give me that crap. If he had farted he'd have parted my hair. Now where in the hell is he?" He bent down to take a long look inside.

50

"Well, you can see for yourself, I'm very much alone," I said, "And I don't think anybody could have jumped out at the speed I was going."

He scratched his head and craned his neck to see better, but the interior of an XKE doesn't afford much room for hiding bodies. He looked understandably perplexed.

"I sure as hell don't see anybody," he said, "But I did see somebody. I saw a guy with his ass up in the air and he was blowing you when you tore past me."

I shrugged. Silence just now seemed the better part of valor. Unfortunately, at that particular moment, Lorin belched.

"Sorry," I said, putting a hand to my mouth. "Something I ate."

The policeman glowered. "I'm beginning to think that's what happened to your buddy," he said. "I've heard of eating a guy, but this is ridiculous….or maybe he really was a fairy, and he just flew away."

"A real fairy could probably just disappear," I said, which produced a faint, muffled laugh from the passenger's seat.

"Yeah? Well, it ain't so goddamn funny," the officer snarled. "Anyway, what in the fuck were you doing driving so fast? I timed you at close to a hundred on the boulevard, wise guy."

"I was just going to bring that up," I said, deciding that my best defense might be a good offense. "I think you people have made that street into a veritable death trap."

"Huh?"

"The way those lights are timed along there. I've tested them out at every possible speed, and I can state without fear of contradiction that the only way to make the lights is at a speed of ninety-eight miles an hour. I think that is ridiculous. The police department ought to be ashamed of themselves, encouraging people to drive at speeds like that. It's unsafe."

"Yeah, it is that," he agreed, a concerned scowl on his face. "Ninety-eight, huh?"

"Ninety-eight and a half, to be exact."

"I never check 'em out," he admitted.

"Well, I think you ought to. I plan on making a big issue out of this. As a matter of fact, I want to get your name and badge number while I'm at it, for my report." I leaned across to the glove box and fumbled around for looking for a piece of paper and a pencil. I found the paper. The pencil got up and put itself in my hand.

"Hey, look," he said, "I ain't got nothing to do with the timing, you understand that? I just patrol this area, see? It ain't my fault if the timing's set wrong."

"Nevertheless, I shall want you full name and badge number," I insisted. He told me, rather reluctantly, and I wrote. I put the paper into my pocket, and gave him my most ingratiating smile. "Don't worry, though," I added, "I'll certainly make mention of how charming and helpful you've been."

"Gee, thanks," he said, positively beaming. "Not too many guys find anything nice to say about us cops."

"Well, I will see that you get the appropriate recognition," I assured him. "Now, if you'll excuse me, I am in a bit of a hurry."

"Oh, sure, hell yes," he said, stepping back from the car. "Look, you want me to give you an escort or anything?"

"Well...." I thought for a moment. "Yes, I guess that would be nice. I do want to get this report filed as quickly as possible."

"Yes, sir," he said, suddenly completely business-like. He gave me a snappy salute and clicked his boots together. "You just follow me."

He marched back to his bike and mounted it. The engine roared to life and a moment later he shot past me, grinning and waving for me to follow. His lights began to blink and his siren wailed.

I pulled out after him and followed in his wake, allowing a certain distance between us. I couldn't help wondering exactly where he was leading me, since we had not discussed destination. Wherever it was, however, I didn't plan to go. Sooner or later he would regain his perspective, and I didn't want to be around when he did.

I gradually let the distance between us widen. While he rushed gallantly onward, I braked suddenly and slid around a corner. I could hear his siren fade into the distance while I circled about to head back from whence I had come.

Lorin materialized beside me. He was clutching his sides and laughing violently. "Mary," he cried, tears streaming down his cheeks. "That was too fucking much!"

His laughter was contagious. I began to giggle myself. It built until in a moment I was laughing so hard that I could scarcely control the car. I was laughing so hard, in fact, that I ran through another stop sign.

This time my luck ran out. I ran smack into the path of a motorcycle officer. I did not need the siren or the lights to tell me that it was my friend, apparently come back to look for me. One glance at his angry face answered all questions for me.

Lorin, of course, only found this all the funnier. He was still laughing when he disappeared again.

*THE GAY HAUNT*, BY VICTOR J. BANIS

# CHAPTER SIX

This time Lorin remained out of sight—and sound—for a while. There was no sign of him during the entire time that I was being taken to the station, booked for reckless driving, and finally released on bail. He still hadn't shown up by the time I got back to where my car was still sitting. Not that I minded, particularly. He was clearly not a good influence on me.

I scowled and thought about my own behavior, and how it changed when he was around. True, it was somewhat the way I had acted in the past. With Lorin around all the time, or a goodly portion of it, I had been considerably less conservative than I was now. I had genuinely thought that I had matured a great deal in the last five years, but it was distressing to see how easily I could revert to being silly and irresponsible.

A good-looking young guy went past while I was stopped at a traffic light. I watched his progress in the crosswalk, checking his basket as he came toward me, and when he had gone by, watching the play of his cute little cheeks in his tight pants. I was still watching when the light changed and somebody behind me honked impatiently.

"Damn," I said aloud, starting off rather too quickly. It was a perfect example of how Lorin influenced me. For years I had been intent on going straight. I couldn't remember when I had last cruised a guy on the street. I had lost all interest in them, as a matter of fact, and if I looked at all, it was at women. So why should I suddenly be looking at baskets and buns just because Lorin was back for a few hours?

Thoughts of the past, however, had given me a destination. I was surprised as I drove toward it to realize how long it had been since I was there. I drove down streets that had once been as familiar as home to me, but now look uncomfortably foreign, like a distant relative ones thinks one remembers, but re-meets, only to find he looks quite different from the image we have retained.

Had the street changed a great deal physically, or had my memories of it been inaccurate? I couldn't say for certain. Here and there, I spotted an obviously new building, or one that had been somewhat remodeled, but not even the little lawns before the houses remained as I remembered them. I suddenly saw the neighborhood as more than a little seedy—but it hadn't been seedy then, when Lorin and I had lived here, had it? Which had changed, me or the neighborhood?

The house in which Lorin and I had lived when we first started together was what romantics call a converted mansion. The fact was, it wasn't anywhere near grand enough ever to have qualified as a mansion. It was only a big, awkward house that had functioned better for having finally been cut up into apartments.

I parked in front and stared at the front porch. No, it had always been slightly tacky looking, I decided. I had only romanticized it in those days, as I had tended to romanticize everything. That was one of the qualities about love that most puzzled me. It colored your perceptions, not just of your lover and your relationship with him. It affected everything else as well. Why should an emotional attachment to another person, for instance, make a steak taste better? But it did, and it made music sound better, and colors seem brighter, and life more fun. Hell, who needed acid when there was love to be loved?

Knock it off, I told myself all of a sudden. That was five years ago, and I was a mature man now, not a silly, mistakenly homosexual jerk. A man of thirty-three had no business being in love, just as he had no need for better tasting steaks or prettier music or brighter colors. There was absolutely nothing wrong with the colors I had been seeing of late.

I was not even sure that Elliot still lived here. His had been the apartment over ours, a bright, open studio ideal for his painting, but it had been almost four years since I had been up to see him.

I frowned when I thought of this. It was odd, actually. Elliot had been my closest friend for a long time. Hell, for a few brief but enjoyable days, he had been a damn sight more than a friend, but that was before Lorin.

When Lorin had come along, I'd had eyes for no one else. Blessedly, Elliot had remained a friend—almost the only person I knew who *did* remain a friend through my "Lorin period." Lorin had managed to eliminate just about everybody else that I had considered friends, replacing them instead with a coterie of his own friends, most of them not much more sensible than he himself was.

Of course, I hadn't seen any of them in years either. I had given all of them up, without any great regrets, when I decided on going straight. Now that I thought about it, though, I did not recall specifically deciding to give up Elliot. If I had considered it, I surely would have decided otherwise, but somehow I had managed to give him up, apparently—or vice versa.

According to the mailbox, which had never been a model of accuracy, Elliot Maxwell still occupied the upstairs studio. I let myself into the foyer. The carpeting hadn't been changed since the old days. What was left of it clung stubbornly to the sagging steps. I remembered better lighting, but after a moment I recalled that Lorin had strung the stairs with Japanese lanterns. He had referred to Elliot's studio as the "tearoom of the sky," because I was inclined to slip up for a cup of tea with Elliot whenever I was disturbed over anything.

Halfway up, without thinking about it, I called, "Anybody home?" the way I used to, without waiting to get to the door and knock.

There was no immediate reply. I was almost to the door, reflecting upon the damn inaccuracy of that mailbox, when the door suddenly opened and an astonished Elliot stood framed in the opening.

If my romance with Lorin had given otherwise shabby items a luster they did not quite deserve, it had had the opposite effect where Elliot was concerned. I had not realized in

57

my memory how handsome he was—not pretty, like Lorin, but handsome. He looked more like a forest ranger than a painter. Just now, he was barefoot, which detracted but little from his six-foot-four height, and the lean rangy body that might have spent all of its forty-odd years out of doors. His hair was unashamedly gray at the temples, his skin tanned dark and leathery. With a tattoo and a cowboy hat, he could have been pushing cigarettes in magazine ads.

I paused when the door opened, and for what must have been a full minute, we just stood still and stared at one another. Then, as if I had only been pint sized, he grabbed me in his arms, lifting me right off the floor in a bear hug that left me gasping for breath.

"Paul," he cried, swinging me around in a circle, "God damn you, you look great. Where the hell have you been? I thought you'd dropped off the end of the world, or something! How are you?"

"Whoa, wait a minute," I said, finally getting my feet back to the floor again. I laughed like a silly queen. It was good seeing Elliot, basking in the warmth of that great big wonderful personality of his. "Let me get my breath back, and I'll try answering a few of those questions."

"Come in, come in," he said, grabbing my arm again and piloting me into the apartment. Inside, in the bright sun that poured through the skylight, he held me away from him and looked me up and down.

"You look great," he pronounced, beaming down on me. "A little gray here and there, but it gives you character."

"You're showing a few years yourself, big fella," I said.

He nodded his head and grimaced. "I'm forty-five. Not much sense worrying about dying my hair when the rest of me shows it."

"Doesn't matter. You look great, too," I assured him. "I just stopped by on an impulse. Hope I'm not interrupting anything."

"Hell, there's nothing so important it can't wait while I have tea with an old friend."

"Sounds great," I said.

"Make yourself at home. I'll put on some water." He disappeared into the tiny kitchen.

"No pretty young things around to share your tea?" I called after him, tossing my jacket across a chair.

"Only one pretty young thing ever shared my tea with me," he called back.

I grinned. Elliot was the only person who had ever categorized me as a pretty young thing. I looked around. The studio didn't seem to have changed at all. I remembered every single chair and table. There was the old beat-up armoire against one wall where he stored his paints and brushes. In the far corner an easel with a canvas mounted on it had been turned to take full advantage of the light. I walked around it to take a look.

It was a shock. It was a literal look into the past. It was a portrait of me. Not me as I looked now, though. Me as I had looked five—no, almost seven years ago, when I had first met Elliot. I stared at the young man in the picture. He was so recognizable and yet so unfamiliar. Had I really had the eyes of a dreamer? I used to smile that way, as though contemplating some private joke of my own? I didn't recognize the expression as mine.

"Like it?" Elliot asked behind me. I jumped. I hadn't heard him come back into the room.

"You did this from memory?" I asked.

He smiled and went to the closet where he kept his finished paintings. He handed out a canvas. It was another painting of me, laughing this time, head back, mouth open wide. I looked incredibly happy. Could I ever have been that happy, I wondered? Had I ever enjoyed life as much as I seemed to there?

There was another one, full length and naked, standing with hips thrust provocatively forward, my cock slightly swollen. He had flattered me, I felt. "I never looked like that," I said.

"Like hell." He propped that picture against the wall and studied it.

"And I never stood like that. I look like a pro getting ready for work."

"You just never saw yourself in that pose," he said.

"Did you?" I was genuinely surprised. It was such an unfamiliar stance.

"Um hum. Every time we ever went to bed together."
He grinned. "You always used to pause, just like that, right
before you climbed into the sack. It was kind of like a hesita-
tion step in dancing. Always drove me wild."

It seemed so very long ago that I had gone to bed with
Elliot. It was one of the things I couldn't even remember
with any clarity. I found myself staring at him, straight
through the faded jeans and plaid shirt he wore. I remembered a long, hard body that smelled vaguely of tobacco and
honest sweat and just a dash of Old Spice. I remembered
strong arms encircling me, dwarfing me, and a worshipful
tenderness that made me feel like the most beautiful, wonderful thing in the world.

We were suddenly both blushing. It seemed as if we
were thinking of the same things. I turned away, but not before I had seen that there were still other pictures of me in
the closet.

"Doesn't seem like a very profitable hobby, painting
pictures of a one time trick." I didn't mean it to sound quite
as flippant as it did.

"I never did things purely for profit," he said. The tea-
kettle began to whistle in the kitchen, and he went to make
tea.

When he came back and we were seated on mammoth
floor pillows, I asked, "Seriously, how have the sales been?"

He shrugged it off as of no consequence. "I keep the rent
paid and the larder stocked," he said. "Plenty of scotch on
hand and plenty of cigarettes. That about covers my needs.
The material ones, anyway. What about you?"

"Oh, I'm doing fine at the firm," I said. "Lots of promo-
tions. I'm in line for a partnership, as a matter of fact." I said
it boastfully, wanting Elliot to be proud of my accomplish-
ments.

"How's the writing?" he asked instead.

"Jesus, I haven't tried to write anything in three or four
years. I've been too busy."

He smiled into his cup. "I remember how we used to sit
and talk about the future, or about art in general. You were
very worried about being able to cultivate your soul, as I recall."

60

I had an uneasy feeling I was being needled about something that I couldn't quite put into words. "I was very young then," I said.

"You're not exactly old now."

I lost my temper unexpectedly. "Damn it," I snapped, flinging a paper napkin on the floor. "First Lorin and then you...."

He shot me a surprised look. "What about Lorin?" he asked.

I had caught myself. I wasn't about to start trying to explain about Lorin, not even to Elliot. Hell, he'd think I was crazy—and for all I knew, maybe I was.

"Nothing," I stammered, trying to recover my poise. "I've just been thinking about him a lot lately, that's all."

He grunted and took a sip of tea. "Bad train of thought, if you ask my opinion."

"You're just prejudiced," I said, although why I should feel the need to defend Lorin was beyond me. "You never liked him when he was alive."

"True. I never made any pretense, either." He was silent for a moment. "Actually," he went on, "It wasn't so much a question of liking or disliking Lorin. He was okay in his way. He was good for a lot of laughs, and taken in small doses he could be downright pleasant—invigorating, you might say. But he sure fucked up your life."

"I don't know about that," I said a little stiffly.

"Shit." It was his turn to crumple up a napkin and give it a toss. "You were nice, just fine, until he came along. You were working hard on your writing, and you were an all around great guy. And then he got hold of you and turned you inside out, and for a long while he led you around with a ring in your nose."

"Granted, I was a little foolish from time to time," I said sharply. "That happens when a guy falls in love. You'd feel different if it had been you I was foolish over."

He stood up quickly, almost knocking over the teapot. "Okay, so I was jealous," he said, walking to the window to stand with his back to me. "I admit it. Hell, you and me, we were a pretty regular pair before he came along. After that, nothing. I haven't even seen you in years."

I was sorry for my last remark. Elliot had been too nice about everything to have his nose rubbed in it now.

"I'm sorry it didn't work out differently," I said, without moving from where I was. "I wish I could have been in love with you. Hell, I don't know, maybe I was. Whatever it was, Lorin eclipsed it. You're right, it would probably have been better if he hadn't, but he did, and there's no undoing that. But I really appreciated the fact that you kept your feelings and your jealousy to yourself, and became a real friend to me, instead of a disappointed lover."

He chuckled softly and shrugged it off. He turned and came back to the big pillow. "Been to the Blue Light lately?" he asked, changing the subject.

I shook my head. "Not in almost five years, since Lorin…passed over." I just couldn't bring myself to say, "died," not with Lorin back in semi-circulation.

He lifted one eyebrow. "Don't tell me there's somebody I don't know about?"

"As a matter of fact," I said, avoiding his inquiring gaze, "There is. That was one of the things I wanted to talk to you about."

For the tiniest fraction of a second there was an expression of disappointment on his face. I was astonished to see how much he still cared. But he chased it away at once, replacing it with an ear-to-ear grin.

"Why, you old son of a bitch, here I'm telling you how I have pined for you all these years, and you've been all settled and married to Mister Right."

"Not exactly," I said, still looking down. "Not yet. I'm going to be married pretty soon, though."

"Well, come on, out with it. Who is he? Anybody I know?"

"I don't think so. As a matter of fact, he isn't a he. He's a she. Her name is Margo. Margo Sellers."

"A girl?" He looked a little puzzled, which was understandable.

"Well, a woman, I mean. See, I gave up the gay scene," I said, talking faster than I intended. "I finally saw that it just wasn't right for me, that I wasn't cut out for it."

62

"Lorin's kind of gay scene wasn't right for you," he said. "Hell, that's what I was just trying to tell you a minute ago. But—married? Heterosexually married? Jesus, that's a big step. You've got to think of her, and kids, if you have any. And your own happiness." I started to say something, but he didn't give me the chance. "Don't misunderstand, I'm not putting down the straight scene. The last thing I'd ever want to do is to try to convert a straight to the queer life. But I don't think it works much better the other way, either, not in the cases I've seen."

"I'm sure," I said, annoyed again. I had come here look-ing for…I wasn't quite sure what. In the past, whenever any-thing had bugged me, just basking in the warmth of Elliot's affection and respect made me feel better. I had an odd feel-ing right now, though, that he disapproved of me. In the past, we had made jokes about the yo-yos, as he called them, the jerks who went through life kidding themselves and never understanding what it was all about. Now, for the first time, I had a feeling that I was on the side of the yo-yos. I had been put there, and I didn't understand why. "I gave it a lot of thought, and I'm convinced this is the right thing for me to do."

He was silent for a moment. Then he gave me a pene-trating look. "Isn't this Sellers girl the boss's daughter?"

"Yes," I said sharply. "But, goddamn it, that hasn't any-thing to do with it. She's a nice girl, and I happened to have fallen in love with her, and you're the last person I expected to look down his nose because I got cured. That's what ho-mosexuality is, you know, a disease." I got up and went to where I had tossed my jacket when I came in.

"Maybe I like being sick," he said, standing also.

"Fine. Stay sick. Just leave me alone."

"I have," he said quietly. "All this time, I've wanted so much to look you up, to tell you I still cared about you, but I thought after Lorin you wanted to be alone for a while. I made myself wait until you were ready to come back here. I guess that is being sick."

I felt ashamed for what I'd said. "I'm sorry," I mumbled. "It's just that, damn it, nobody takes me seriously. I waited a long time because I wanted a chance to test it, to see if my hunch was right. I couldn't have decided I was straight if I had the gay scene in front of me to tempt me all the time."

"I shouldn't think it would tempt a straight guy," he said.

He suddenly came across the room, taking long, surprisingly graceful steps, and before I knew what was happening, I was in his arms again. He kissed me. He kissed me like the fleet had just landed.

To my surprise, it was nice. Even more to my surprise, I felt a slight stirring in my pants. Hell, I thought Lorin had drained that thing dry, but there was still some life there, it seemed. And I didn't like the idea that males seemed to have so little trouble getting it up.

By the time he finally let me go, I was wondering if the Republicans were still in office. He smiled down at me and said, "You sure kiss nice, for a straight man."

I couldn't decide whether to punch him in the nose or stamp my foot—so I did neither. Instead, I said, "Fuck yourself," and left, sending the door crashing back against the wall.

His baritone laugh echoed down the stairs after me. "That's what I've been doing for six years," he called.

# CHAPTER SEVEN

It was not until I was in my car again and on my way home that Lorin reappeared. This time I was happy to note that he had clothes on. In a pair of snug fitting jeans and a body shirt, he looked like a normal human being. Not ordinary—Lorin could never look quite ordinary—but at least he looked human and not like a naked ghost.

"I'm glad you finally got dressed," I greeted him when he popped into sight.

"I thought you might be," he said.

A thought crossed my mind. "I discarded all of your things years ago. Where did those come from?"

"I wandered around while you were with Elliot. There's a cute chick in the downstairs rear apartment, and she had just picked up some guy in the park. So, while they were occupied, I borrowed his clothes."

"What's he going to do when he gets out of bed?"

"From the way he was going, that won't be a problem for quite some time," Lorin said.'

I knew there was no point in trying to appeal to his morality. He had none in the past, and five dead years hadn't improved the matter.

"So you were with me at Elliot's," I said instead. "I thought you'd given up on and gone back to mind your own business."

"I'm with you all the time," he replied, which was not a particularly comforting announcement. "Or nearly all. Except when I get bored. There was nothing for me to do at the police station, so I sort of cruised around for a while."

"You might have tried helping me out of that jam you got me into," I said, my pique renewed at being reminded of that incident. "It was your bare body that got me into that."

"Just my balls," he said.

"What do you mean?"

"The policeman especially noted my bare balls hanging out of the window. Although actually, he was in error. I did fart, and it didn't do a thing to his hair."

"Frankly, I'm not interested in your farting or not farting," I informed him.

"I should hope not. Fetishes are such a bore. Although I can imagine various positions in which you might be interested in my *not*...."

"Change the subject," I said.

"If there's anything I hate, loathe and despise, it's a policeman who exaggerates the charges."

"The charges were quite enough as it was. I cost me a pretty penny to get out of jail."

"You didn't tell Elliot about me?" Lorin had no difficulty in changing subjects without warning.

"No, of course not," I said.

"That's what I thought. That was the only reason I went in at all. I thought if you did it might be kind of campy to watch his reaction, but after you'd fiddled around for a time I decided nothing interesting was going to happen there, so I cut out. My, Elliot is a dull piece, isn't he?"

"I don't think of Elliot as a 'piece,' as you so crudely put it," I said, "And I don't find him dull."

"Oy." He scooted down in his seat, putting his spine into what any chiropractor would consider an impossible position. "That one always bored the tits off me. He's stuffy and quiet and sensible. With all your talk about stables, I'm surprised you didn't marry him."

"I almost did, at one time," I said thoughtfully. I added quickly, "Back when I was still gay."

"Back when cats still had asses," he said. "I think I'd almost rather see you marry the split-tail. At least she's still young enough, there might still be a chance of bringing her to life. But Elliot, he's set for the rest of his years, diddling himself in that studio, reading poetry, going to an occasional concert—and for kicks, he gets out a new canvas and paints another portrait of you. I must say, though, he was right about that nude one. You did always pose like that just before hitting the hay." He turned to grin at me. "You were a sexy bastard."

It was hard not to grin back. "Were?"

He put a hand on my leg. "Still are. If I were alive, I'd go after you again."

The remark erased my grin. I pushed the hand away. "I don't want to repeat that incident," I said. "Anyway, for once you're going to get your wish, because I am going to marry the split-tail…I mean, Margo."

"We'll see," he said, smiling still.

I turned into the driveway and parked the car. "Now look," I said, getting out my side, "I don't want any…."

Lorin was already out of the car, ignoring my protests as usual. "Hello, Mr. Vinson," he called to my neighbor, waving gaily. "I hope your wife is feeling better."

Mr. Vinson waved back and squinted, trying to make out who was with me. I suddenly remember that Lorin was dead and Mr. Vinson knew it. I moved quickly to block his view, giving silent thanks for Mr. Vinson's poor eyesight.

"She's not well," Mr. Vinson said, clucking his tongue. "Not well at all."

"Probably a vitamin deficiency," Lorin called back as I shoved him through the front door. "I recommend aspirin and plenty of orange juice." I closed the door on Mr. Vinson's reply.

"Damn it," I said, "I wish you'd remember that you are dead."

"And I wish you'd stop referring to me in that manner," he replied. "Your girlfriend's genitals are dead. Elliot's dick is dead. And if you go through with your wedding plans, you will be a dead duck. But I am not now, never have been and never will be, dead."

How does one argue with a ghost who insists he isn't dead? I didn't try. Instead, I headed for the bar. I needed a drink badly. "Do ghosts—live ghosts—drink?" I asked him.

"Spirits for the spirits," he said. "I don't know. Let's try a gin on the rocks."

I fixed him a long one, and a straight scotch for me. I was just adding lemon peel to both when the doorbell rang.

"I'll bet it's that nice Mr. Vinson," Lorin cried delightedly, turning toward the door.

"Oh, no you don't," I said, grabbing his arm. "You vanish, right now."

"I will not," he said indignantly.

"Oh, yes you will. If you don't, I'll...I'll marry Margo tomorrow."

"You can't. It takes longer than that."

"We'll elope. We'll run off to Mexico."

He screwed up his face in a grimace, but he shrugged and disappeared, leaving me clasping a handful of air. "Don't say anything nasty," he said from somewhere above me. "I haven't gone far."

I was almost to the door when he suddenly reappeared, almost making me drop my drink. "It isn't Mr. Vinson at all," he said in an excited whisper, "It's that divine Don Clayton."

"Who?"

"Don Clayton. We met him a couple of times at parties, mixed parties. But I always secretly thought he was a member of the club. If I lived a little longer, I was going to find out."

It was not exactly pleasant being reminded of the fact that nothing short of the grave could have kept Lorin from cheating on me. I did remember who Don Clayton was, though. As a matter of fact, he was Margo's cousin. That was how I had met her. Don brought her to a cocktail party that I attended. And I, too, had had a few doubts about the good looking young man, and once almost put myself to resolving the question, but Lorin had been too freshly deceased at the time. Later, I had been involved with Margo, and out of the gay life, so the question had never been answered, and no longer particularly mattered.

"You still have to vanish," I insisted, also speaking in a whisper. The doorbell rang again impatiently. "He knows you. Knew you, I mean."

"Well, how on earth can I arrange anything with him if I have to be invisible?" he pouted.

"Wait until he dies," I said. "Now, go, please."

"That could take years," he said. He put a finger to his mouth. "Unless…."

"Now stop that," I said, giving him a shove. For all I knew, Lorin might be perfectly capable of speeding up Don's crossover.

The doorbell rang again. "I'm not going to open it until you've vanished," I warned him, "And you'll never get a crack at him."

"Oh." He shot me an angry glance, but he disappeared again.

I knew Don Clayton only slightly, and I hadn't seen him in a long time. I was surprised, when I opened the door, to realize how really good looking he was. More than that, I experienced a shock of recognition. He looked astonishingly like Lorin. They were similar of build and general features, both blond, both pretty. There was a certain air of mischief in Don's quick grin and sparkling eyes that aroused a spark of desire within me, yet made me wary at the same time. What I did not need was another madcap.

"Hi," he greeted me, flashing what appeared to be more than the normal consignment of teeth. "I'm Don Clayton, Margo's cousin. Remember?"

"Of course I remember," I said. "How are you?"

"Groovy." He was trying, none too discreetly, to peer past me into the apartment. "Are you *occupé*? You know, busy?"

"No, no, I'm quite by myself," I said, hoping as I said it that I still was. There was no telling when Lorin might change his mind and come back. For all I knew, he might be peering over my shoulder right now.

"Can I come in?" Don asked, since I was still blocking the doorway.

There wasn't any way of tactfully refusing, especially since I had just said that I was alone, but it was with some misgiving that I said, "Oh, sure," and stepped aside.

He gave the living room a sweeping glance. "It took you such a long time to answer the door," he said.

"I was…." I had to think for a moment. "I was on the john. Some things you just can't cut short."

"I thought I heard voices," he said.

"Voices?"

"You know, while I was waiting. Whispery voices. I thought you had somebody here and didn't want me to know about it because of my being Margo's cousin and all."

"No, I'm completely alone," I insisted. I managed a slight chuckle. "Anyway, I couldn't know it was you out there, could I?"

He shrugged. That question seemed a little too weighty for him. He was not, now that I thought of it, overly loaded upstairs. Of course, with his body and his face, that wasn't a tragedy.

"Because, I don't tell Margo everything," he went on blithely. "Heavens, I wouldn't dare. If she knew the details of my private life, she'd be horrified." He gave me a conspiratorial wink. "So you don't have to worry about my telling her anything about *your* really private life. My lips are sealed."

"That must interfere with some of your social activities," I pointed out.

He giggled and looked coy. "Oh, Paul, what a wild thing to say, and we hardly know one another."

"I was thinking of things like talking and drinking coffee," I said quickly.

"But now that we understand one another," he continued as if he hadn't heard me, "Things are going to be much more interesting."

"Anyway," I said, ignoring the leads he was giving me, "I don't have any private life. Not that Margo doesn't share, anyway. Oh." I jumped. Someone had goosed me. I looked over my shoulder, but he was still invisible.

"What's wrong?" Don asked, giving me a curious look.

"Nothing's wrong," I said. "Why?"

"You jumped like somebody had goosed you."

I forced a laugh. "That's hardly possible, unless you believe in ghosts." I slapped away another poke in the direction of my ass.

"I don't know," he said, making an apparent attempt at thought. "You're all the time hearing about live people who turn dead. I don't see why dead people couldn't turn live. Isn't that a scientific law, every opposite has its other side?"

"Something like that," I said, starting for the bar. "Can I get you a drink?"

"Why do you have two?" he asked.

"Two what?"

"Two drinks. There's one in your hand there, a brownish one, and one on the bar, that isn't brownish."

I had forgotten Lorin's non-brownish gin, sitting on the bar. I went over quickly and picked it up. "That's the way I always drink," I said, grinning. "A gin, with scotch on the side." To prove my point, I took a sip of the gin and followed it with a big gulp of the scotch. The two had an unpleasant confrontation somewhere en route to my stomach.

He gave me another curious look. I winked over the top of the gin glass and he smiled and shrugged. "I guess you get there twice as fast," he said. "I'll have a martini."

"Here, have this," I said, holding the glass of gin toward him. "It's the next thing, without the vermouth and the garnish, is all."

He shook his head. "No point in spoiling your drinking fun," he said. "Unless you're out of liquor?"

"Oh, no, there's plenty." I took another sip of each drink—they seemed to blend together better this time—and went around the bar to fix him a martini. "Twist?" I inquired when the glass was filled.

"By myself?" he asked, looking puzzled

"I see your point," I said, and dropped a twist of lemon peel into his glass. "Here, try this."

He took a long sip. "Umm, it taste's like gin," he said.

"It is gin."

"Well, wasn't that a clever guess," he said with a pleased expression.

I tried, but it didn't make much sense. "Here's how," I said, toasting him with both my glasses.

"I already know how," he said. I was prepared to concede that point, although I suspected that was the limit of his knowledge. He lifted his glass. "Here's looking up your address."

"A tender sentiment," I muttered, taking another drink from each of my glasses. The gin and the scotch were definitely tasting better together now.

"How about some music?" Don asked, spying the stereo.

"Sure, flip it on. There's some Mantovani on the turntable."

"Nothing classical for me, thanks. Where's your records at?"

"Against the wall," I said, pointing. "Take your pick."

"Thanks. Could I have another one of these?" He handed me his cocktail glass, that had somehow miraculously gotten empty.

"That's pretty fast drinking," I said, staring wide-eyed at the glass.

"Now, now." He wagged a finger at me. "I'm only drinking one at a time, so I'll have to try harder to be number two."

"I see." Strangely, his remarks were beginning to make a little sense. I finished off my drinks too, and set about mixing a fresh batch—a martini for him, a martini for me, and a scotch on the rocks for me. I took a long look at my two glasses, decided they were inconvenient, and dumped both drinks into one oversize tumbler. It tasted a little weird, but it made for freer hands.

Other hands were getting freer, too. Don bent over slightly to get a closer look at some of the books in the case—not that I imagined for a moment that he could read the titles. Suddenly he squealed and straightened up, turning around with a big smile on his face.

"Naughty, naughty," he said, wagging his finger again. "Feel if you like but don't pinch."

I swallowed and looked chagrined. "I'll remember," I promised.

"I don't mind the feeling part," he explained, just in case I had been too discouraged. "I get excited."

I lifted my glass again. "Here's to excitement," I said.

# CHAPTER EIGHT

"To excitement," he said in return. He drained his glass and handed it to me for a refill. I had a feeling there would be plenty of excitement before this day was ended. And the way I was beginning to feel, I didn't much give a rat's ass. I figured I had a good drunk coming. I had already earned it. I made a fresh martini for Cute Little Don, and a new gin and scotch for me, extra tall. I couldn't remember when I had ever had a drink quite so refreshing. It was really a spectacularly good mixture of flavors.

"I'm so glad we got things straightened out between us," Don said, taking the fresh glass with a giggle and crinkling up his adorable little nose.

"Did we?" I asked, wrinkling my nose right back at him.

"Didn't we?" His turn to crinkle.

"About what?"

"About your being gay, too," he said, exchanging crinkles for winks

"Who says I am?" I asked, sobering slightly. I had just remembered that this was Margo's cousin. Anyway, whatever he was, I wasn't. Not anymore at least, although I didn't want to try to explain that distinction to him.

"I do. I'm what they call extra-sensory. I get information without knowing anything." He seemed rather proud of this peculiar attribute.

"And what if I say I'm not?" I didn't like being pegged for queer just like that, without a by-your-leave. I was just as straight as the next one.

"You're so cute when you're drunk," he said for a reply. He took my face in both of his hands, stretched up a little, and kissed me full on the mouth. I couldn't think just what to do, so I kissed him back. It wasn't such a bad experience, so I did it again.

"What if I say I'm not gay?" I repeated when we took a break from kissing.

"Lights," he said.

"Huh?"

"We need lights. It's getting dark. Unless you want to just stay in the dark." He giggled.

I looked around. To my surprise, he was right. It was getting dark. I tried to think of the reason. An eclipse of the sun? I didn't remember having any scheduled. Too many gin and scotches? Possible, but I didn't remember blacking out before. Besides, he was experiencing it too.

I looked at my watch. It was several hours fast. It read seven o'clock already, when I knew it couldn't be anywhere near that late. I tried to do a mental run through of the day, but it was a little blurred. All that running in the car, with Lorin's ass sticking out, and then a couple of hours, maybe three, at the police station. A visit to Elliot's. And—how many drinks?

"My God," I said, looking at my watch again. "It really is seven thirty."

"So?"

"Margo."

"Don't be silly. I'm not Margo, I'm Don."

I pushed him away. "I know that. I meant, I was supposed to call Margo about dinner."

"Well, what about me?" he asked, assuming a pouty pose.

"Fix yourself another drink," I told him. I headed for the stairs, thinking it might be best to use the upstairs phone.

Lorin was at my side by the time I reached the top of the stairs. I noticed first thing that he had gotten rid of the clothes again. I took that for an ominous sign.

"I thought you weren't interested in him," he said, lifting one eyebrow.

"I'm not," I said, adding, "Exactly."

"You weren't fighting him off, either—exactly," he pointed out.

"He's aggressive. And he reminds me of you."

74

"You're right, he is a lot like me, isn't he? Only I was brighter."

"I wonder," I said. "You don't suppose that dumb routine could be just an act?"

"Not even the Barrymores could act that well," Lorin said. "But I don't think he's dumb when it comes to getting his man."

"He hasn't gotten this one yet, if that's what you're hinting at."

"Why fight him, though. You said yourself, he reminds you a lot of me. And he is a little doll baby. I'm sure he'd be absolutely wild in bed."

I stopped and gave him a suspicious look. "Why this sudden interest in seeing me having a good time in the sack—with someone else?"

He gave an innocent shrug. "I want to convince you not to marry that female, by any means." He pursed his lips. "Besides, I wouldn't mind a piece of that myself."

"I thought there was something like that to it. And I've already told you, you have to stay invisible."

"That's what I mean. I'm only trying to think of ways to save you embarrassment."

Conversation with Lorin wasn't much clearer than conversation with Don. "How do you mean?" I asked.

"Well, the way I see it, if he were a little drunker, and the two of you were in bed, and you had him quite occupied—I mean, how would he be expected to know if someone else had joined the fun?"

"If he's blowing me and somebody shoves a cock up his ass, I expect he'd know it wasn't mine," I said.

"I'm not so sure."

"Forget it. And be quiet, I'm going to phone Margo."

"It isn't necessary," he said. "I already did."

"You did what?" I stared at him in disbelief. The prospect of Lorin and Margo having a conversation was more than my befuddled brain was ready to accept.

"Now, don't get all panicky," he said. "I didn't talk to her directly. I just left a message from you, saying that you were tied up on a business proposition and would call her tomorrow."

I slammed my hand down on the telephone. "Of all the nerve...!"

He remained unalarmed by my anger. "It was pretty much the truth," he said. "At the moment, you were being propositioned. And such a business."

"I'll thank you to keep his business out of my business," I said. "And your nose out of both businesses."

"Does that mean you're not going to help fix me up with him?"

"You're damned right it does," I assured him, starting back toward the stairs.

"Then I'll have to act on my own," he said, and was gone before I could protest.

"Damn it, come back here," I snapped, lowering my voice, although in my absence Don had turned the stereo up so loud that I could have fired an elephant gun with no fear of being heard.

Lorin appeared in front of me. "Make up your mind," he said. "Earlier you were demanding that I leave."

"I just want to get things straight."

"I don't see how you could," he said. "Yours has a distinct curve to it, upward at about a...."

"I want you to disappear and stay disappeared," I said. "That's what I wanted to get straight."

"But I had disappeared."

"I just wanted to make sure you did." I turned on my heel and started downstairs again, thinking that I never had been able to come out ahead in an argument with Lorin.

Don had made himself at home in my absence. And apparently, at home he wore very little. His clothes were scattered about the room in various heaps and he was dancing to the numbing beat of the rock music from the stereo, wearing nothing more than an incredibly brief pair of bikini shorts.

It was, even to a man who had gone straight, a highly stimulating sight. His body was lithe and little-boyish. He looked sleek and supple, twisting and bending to the music, his slim hips undulating and swaying with each movement, his blond hair tossing as he threw his head to and fro. The cleavage between his ass cheeks began above the top of his briefs and disappeared beneath the thin fabric, becoming instead an alluring shadow that drew the eye down between those delectable mounds. His skin was pale, his body virtually hairless except for the suggestion of down that could be seen high up on his thighs, just disappearing into the brief.

I stared and swallowed a lump that had appeared in my throat, and tried to remind myself that this was Margo's cousin, and I was engaged to Margo, and I had given up boys forever.

It got harder to remember any of that when he turned and saw me watching. He grinned and began to dance over to where I stood. His genitals were a tempting little mound in the front of the briefs, jiggling and bouncing with each step. His belly button invited a tongue's invasion. His belly was nonexistent. His nipples were nibble material. I swallowed harder. For that matter, I *got* harder.

"Hi," he said in a whisper when he was right in front of me. I was certain I could feel the heat radiating from his body.

"Hi," I croaked back.

"Can I ask you a question?" he wanted to know.

I thought of all sorts of possible questions. How big was my meat? Was I horny? Would I like to fuck him?

"Shoot," I said, close to doing just that myself.

"What's all this about Lorin?" he asked.

*THE GAY HAUNT*, BY VICTOR J. BANIS

# CHAPTER NINE

I stared in silence for quite a long time, thinking of what I ought to say. All I needed was for Lorin to pop into view at just that moment, but fortunately, he didn't.

"What about Lorin?" I asked finally, managing a rather wan smile.

"That's what I was wondering," he said, only barely swaying now in time to the music. "That's why I came over today. That, and because I wanted to get better acquainted with you."

"I don't follow you," I said. I went to the bar and poured myself a fast drink, concentrating on scotch this time. This was no occasion for cutting one's liquor.

"Margo called me," he explained. "She said you had been acting peculiar. Then she said that you had called her Lorin a couple of times. She thought maybe as another man, I could offer some sort of explanation."

"Margo's rather naïve," I said, emptying my glass.

He ignored that remark, if he even heard it. "Of course, I remembered right off who Lorin was. I had always suspected you two were more than just friends. And he was such a doll. I was always gaga over him."

"I think it was mutual," I said, finishing the rest of the scotch.

He sighed dreamily. "Pity he had to go. Think what fun we'd have if he were with us tonight."

"Don't say that," I snapped rather quickly.

He shrugged. "Anyway, I got to thinking about your being engaged to marry Margo, and you suddenly calling her by Lorin's name, when you're in bed together, and I wondered if you weren't having misgivings. I mean, like maybe you were in just the right mood for a fling. So I told Margo I'd come over and have a chat with you, just to see what came up. Of course, I didn't explain to her exactly how I meant that remark."

"Damn good of you," I muttered. The Scotch bottle was empty. I switched back to gin.

"So?"

That seemed to be a question, but I wasn't following him clearly enough to make sense of it. "So?" I echoed.

"So, what about Lorin? Has your engagement brought him back, so to speak?"

"So to speak," I answered, nodding.

"That's just what I suspected." He gave me what was seemingly a sympathetic look. His sympathy wasn't confined just to looks, though. I discerned movement further down and peered in that direction. He had hooked his thumbs into the elastic of his briefs. While I stared wide-eyed, he tugged gently downward, peeling then down over his narrow hips, bending slightly to push them further. They fell about his feet and he stepped out of them.

It was what Lorin used to call a "pretty peter." Not particularly big, just pretty and fresh and delicious looking. I did not have long to look at it, though. The view was hampered by the fact that he came against me, putting his arms around me.

"Let me comfort you," he said in a baby voice, lifting his face so I could kiss him. I did, against my better judgment. I had promised myself I wouldn't put my arms about him, but they somehow got there of their own accord. My hands, which I ordered to get into my pockets and stay there, slid instead along the smooth skin of his back, down to those soft, yielding mounds. I cupped them longingly, tracing the line of that warm crevice with the tip of one finger. It was quite fortunate, I thought, that Marge was not here for the evening.

Margo! That thought did finally get through. I gulped and broke off our embrace, not exactly an easy feat. He gave me a startled look.

"Stand right there," I said, giving him my sternest look. "Don't move a muscle." His cock, which of course by this

80

time was standing straight out before him, jumped. "Not even that," I said, pointing at it.

I was, I knew, drunker than I had ever been in my life, and I felt it was wise to get just a little drunker. I went to the bar, filled a glass with gin, and half emptied it in one long gulp. I came back to where he was standing at the foot of the stairs. "Keep standing there," I told him, going right on by him.

"Where are you going?" he called up after me.

"I'm going to lock myself in my room," I told him without pausing. "You'll find an unlocked door that is to the guest bedroom. Make yourself as comfortable as you like, in *that* room."

"But, aren't you going to…to do anything?" he wailed.

"Yes. I'm going to sleep until I'm sober."

Lorin appeared just as I locked my door securely. To be extra, extra certain, I pushed the dresser in front of the door too.

"Have you gone crazy?" he demanded.

"I almost did," I said angrily, not looking at him. All I needed was another naked body trying to stir me up. "You almost made me forget that I don't go that route anymore. Almost, but not quite."

"And what about that pretty little thing downstairs?"

"For all I care you can stick him up your ass," I snapped, finishing the gin I had brought with me. "That's about what you had in mind, isn't it?"

In the bathroom I shook a sleeping pill out of the bottle in my hand, contemplated it for a moment, and added another. It was a certainty that I was going to sleep. I stumbled drunkenly back into the bedroom. Lorin had gone. Probably, I thought, taking my suggestion literally. At this particular moment, I didn't care if the appearance of a ghost scared little Don out of his pants—which, of course, he was long since out of anyway.

It wasn't so easy to stop thinking about my guest, though. Even when the room had started spinning around, I could still see that pretty little butt wriggling in front of me, and that tempting cock. Except for the size of the cock, he did look frighteningly like Lorin. In my imagination, he was standing by the bed, and he looked more and more like Lorin. The room was mostly dark, so it was hard to tell. I reached for his cock, and realized it *was* Lorin. If I was going to have an erotic dream, I thought it was probably just as well to have it of Lorin and not some newcomer. It wasn't quite as gay that way, or so it seemed to me.

Lorin bent down in my dream, kissing me lightly and affectionately on the lips. "I want to be certain you sleep well," he whispered, sliding into bed alongside me.

"Not necessary," I mumbled drunkenly. But of course, this wasn't just an ordinary dream, it was an erotic fantasy, so something erotic had to happen. I wasn't altogether displeased when Lorin began to kiss his way along the length of my body, touching upon all the more vulnerable spots.

By the time he got to my prick, that overworked instrument was hard again. I hadn't had this much sexual stimulation since Lorin had choked on that damned diamond and departed from me. With Margo and me, it was maybe once a week or so. I had attributed that to my growing older, but just now I didn't feel terribly old.

His tongue flicked at the head and along the sensitive underside. His lips slid along the rigid shaft. He licked my balls, which never fails to turn me on, and followed the ridge behind them, lifting my leg over his shoulder to enable him to rim me. As dreams went, this was a very pleasant one, I found myself thinking.

He went back to my cock. It was fortunate in one respect that this was a dream. I was certain that I would never be able to come, having shot one load today and with all the drinking I had done.

He was doing a good job, though, making it so realistic that it soon felt as if I really was going to come. It was so real, in fact, that I had begun to fuck his willing mouth in earnest, pumping in and out while he caressed my ass and my balls and my thighs, and sucked like crazy the whole time. My balls had begun to ache with their weight, and I felt that wonderful surge within me, and suddenly, I was shooting, blowing a load into that heavenly sucking, licking, gulping mouth—and it was hard to believe it was only a dream.

With the last spurt, I surrendered to the darkness that had been waiting for me.

*THE GAY HAUNT*, BY VICTOR J. BANIS

# CHAPTER TEN

I woke to the accompaniment of excruciating pain. For several long moments I left my eyes closed and contemplated the agony I was suffering. It was entirely possible, I reasoned, that I had died during the night and was already in hell. Or perhaps I was the victim of some modern day de Sade, who already had me on the rack. I moved a tentative hand, then an arm. They seemed free enough. I moved the other hand and arm, and both feet.

Finally I opened my eyes. The light was like a hammer whacking me on the top of the skull. I closed the eyes for a moment, although the situation was not much better when I opened them the second time.

It took several tries to get to a sitting position, and another good ten minutes before I had gotten my feet planted on the floor and was able to stand. Clinging rather desperately to the wall, I was finally able to reach the bathroom.

I was downing the third aspirin when Lorin appeared with a glass containing a dubious looking concoction. "Good morning," he greeted me with altogether painful cheer. "How are we feeling this morning?

"Like the entire Russian army marched through my bedroom with their pants down," I informed him. "And about half of them paused to shit in my mouth." I gargled with mouthwash but the brown taste lingered on.

"Drink this," he said, offering me the glass. "It's guaranteed to pick you up."

"And put me down where?" I asked, looking warily at the contents of the glass.

"Now, now, no retorts. Up to the lips and over the gums, watch out stomach, here she comes." He lifted my hand with the glass toward my lips. I was confident that nothing could make me feel worse, so I took a long swallow.

My confidence was misguided. Drinking Lorin's cure was vaguely akin to vomiting in reverse. I shifted gears and brought it all back up, just making it to the toilet bowl in time.

"Jesus H. Christ," I gasped after a few minutes. "What was in that?"

"One part vodka, one part bourbon, one part rum, two raw eggs, a clove of garlic, a generous dollop of Worcestershire sauce and a dash of rubbing alcohol," he explained.

"Where in God's name did you get that recipe? From The Pharmacist's Guide to Lethal Poisons?"

"From a man on the other side. He said it was guaranteed to cure a hangover." He pursed his lips in thought. "Now that I think of it, though, I believe he died from it."

"I shouldn't wonder." I rinsed my mouth out again and started replacing the aspirin I had just lost. Memory was beginning to return. "What happened to our little friend? " I asked.

"He's asleep in the guest room. He looks just like a little lamb when he sleeps."

I gave him a suspicious look. "You didn't pull anything after I conked out, did you?" I asked.

He assumed a wounded posture. "Please, this is the face of a woman you can trust."

"It's a face I can trust to create all sorts of trouble for me. Come on, let me have it."

He put his hand up in a scout pledge. "I give you my word of honor, he remains blissfully unaware of my existence," he said.

"Okay, just keep it that way." I got a robe from my closet and unlocked my door. The extra bedroom was almost directly across the hall. Don was sprawled naked across the surface of the bed. Even in my hung over condition I could not help noticing what an attractive little thing he was. Fortunately, I was sober this morning, and my appreciation of his charms was purely aesthetic.

He opened his eyes as I paused in the doorway and sent a broad smile my way. "Good morning," he said, stretching and seeming almost to purr. "I hope you've brought my breakfast under that robe."

"There's nothing under the robe but me, I'm afraid," I said.

His smile grew. "That's just what I had in mind."

"I'm afraid that's out of the question," I told him coolly.

He pouted and reached with one hand to rub his bare ass. "Gosh, that sure is sore this morning," he said.

"From what?" I asked innocently. I hope he hadn't hurt himself dancing.

He giggled and fluttered his eyelashes. "Oh, you are such a camp," he said. "As if you didn't know."

"I'm afraid I *don't* know."

"You know, I'm usually pretty good at guessing size," he said, "But you fooled me. I wasn't sure I could take that much. But it was sheer heaven."

All of a sudden, a light came on in my mind. "You got fucked last night," I said.

"I certainly did," he replied, giving his ass cheek a gentle pat. "You tiger, you."

I nearly told him that he had the wrong tiger by the tail, but I checked myself in time. "Glad you enjoyed it," I muttered. "I think you had better get up and get dressed. It's late."

"I'm already up," he said. He rolled over on his back to confirm the remark. His cock was standing rigidly. "Shouldn't we do something about that?"

"I'd suggest taking a leak," I said, and went back to my own room, slamming the door hard. Lorin came into view, seated on one corner of the bed.

"Now, there's no reason to be angry," he said before I could make any comments. "I promised you he didn't know anything about my existence, and he doesn't. He thought it was you, and I just didn't bother to correct that impression."

"'Thanks a hell of a lot," I said, getting into my clothes. "All I need is for Margo's cousin to tell her he got fucked by me."

"Which he is hardly likely to do. Besides, you ought to try it yourself. He's downright heavenly. And I should know."

"Get lost," I said, fastening my belt and starting from the room. "Preferably permanently."

Don was not in bed. The door to the guest bathroom was open. I stepped inside. The shower was running, telling me where he was. I started to leave when I caught sight of his silhouette against the shower door.

I was suddenly struck by the beauty of the male body—not just his body, but the lines and curves of the male body in general. I had never thought of it like that before. Always before there had been a particular body—Lorin's, Elliot's, or one of several others. I had credited my liking for the body to my interest in that particular person. Ergo, I would turn straight by falling in love with a female, whose body would then turn me on.

It wasn't the same thing, though. I did care for Margo, and we were satisfactory in bed, but I suddenly realized that her body lacked the lean grace of the one beyond the shower door—but if it was the male body in general that I loved, then how could I turn straight?

I forced my eyes away from the shower and my thoughts aware from these questions. No doubt I was just suffering a lingering case of the "hots," brought on by his nude, lewd dancing of the night before. After all, it wasn't necessary that you be queer to be turned on by the sight of naked flesh.

I left the bathroom, assuming my guest would be able to find his own way downstairs for coffee—perhaps a rather generous assumption in view of his apparent limitations in the area of brainpower.

I didn't quite make it to the kitchen. The doorbell rang just as I was crossing the dining area. "Who?" I asked myself as I came back to the door.

It was Margo. She looked, I thought, disgustingly fresh and unspoiled. I consider two things most aggravating: people who are hung over when I am not, and people who are not when I am. I kept these thoughts to myself, however.

"Margo," I said, staring and doing my best not to look hung over. "What a surprise."

"I'm sure it must be," she said, giving her words a razor sharp edge. "It's been so long since last we met. May I come in?"

"Of course, don't be silly," I said, dancing out of the way to hold the door for her.

She came in with chin high, eyes flicking about for any suspicious sights. "I thought since you won't come to see me that I might try coming to you," she said.

"Margo, I'm sorry about last night," I said rather lamely. I was thinking about something else, though. I was wondering how long Don normally spent in the shower. I did not have long to wonder. A second or two later, the shower door crashed open with a bang. Margo's eyes crashed open too, and threatened to do some banging of their own.

"Margo, I think I'd better explain something," I said quickly.

"I think you should," she said. "No, on second thought, I don't think I care for your explanations. I think I would like to see for myself." She strode past me toward the stairs.

"Margo," I spoke vainly, following after her, "You don't understand…."

"Don't be so sure," she said, without slowing her pace. She marched up the stairs like a general reviewing the troops. All I could do was follow her into the battle zone.

She went toward my bedroom first, but a sudden sound from the guest room brought her about and she went to that door instead. I had pulled it closed when I came out. She reached for the knob, and then pulled her hand back.

"Open that door," she said to me in a voice that was little more than a hiss.

"Margo," I tried again.

"Open it!" It was not a tone of voice to encourage further discussion. With a helpless nod of my head, I turned the knob and pushed the door open.

The view was rather spectacular. We were, for all practical purposes, looking up Don's rather inviting asshole. At the sound of the door, he straightened and turned. His cock was only slightly softer than it had been before. It stood out before him, pointing in my direction like an accusing finger.

He flashed a bright smile, first at me and then at Margo. "Hi, cuz," he said, in what I thought was an extremely nonchalant manner.

*THE GAY HAUNT*, BY VICTOR J. BANIS

## CHAPTER ELEVEN

"What are you doing here?" Margo demanded, more than a little nonplussed.

"I just finished taking a shower," he said. If he was at all embarrassed by his nudity or his erection, he gave no sign of it. He looked around for his cigarettes, found them on the nightstand, and lit one. I found myself admiring his sleek body once again.

"I was under the impression," Margo said, "That you had bathing facilities at your own apartment."

"I do," he admitted, all wide-eyed innocence, "But you wouldn't expect me to go all the way across town like this, would you?"

"I frankly don't understand what you're doing in this condition anyway," Margo said, growing cooler.

Don glanced down at his cock. "You mean like this? It's always like this in the morning, unless someone does something about it."

"I was referring to your nakedness, not your state of sexual excitation," Margo said.

"Oh, I don't have any excitation," he assured her. "It's just that I'm horny. I always am in the morning. I need someone to take care of it."

"Well, I am the only female in the place, and I have no intention of accommodating you," she said in her frostiest tones. "If there is no alternative, I would suggest you try auto manipulation."

He looked highly doubtful. "Gee, I don't even drive, Margo, you know that. I thought I'd just catch a cab later, you know."

"I am talking about driving your...." She shook her head in a flustered manner. "I'm not talking about driving at all, for Pete's sake. Will you put some clothes on? I'm going downstairs." She whirled about and marched from the room.

"I still wish someone would take care of it for me," Don said, with a wink in my direction, which I ignored.

"Get some clothes on," I said, following Margo. In a much lower voice, just in case anyone was lurking close at hand, but unseen, I added, "And don't you give him any help with his problem."

Margo was standing at the living room window, staring out. I came up behind her and put my arms around her. She stiffened and tried to pull away, but I held her firmly against me.

"What I don't understand," she said, "Is what on earth my cousin is doing traipsing around naked in your house."

"He led me to believe you sent him over," I said. "To have a man-to-man talk."

"Well," she said, melting slightly, "I did ask him about you, but I still don't see...."

"We had a nice long man-to-man talk last night," I said. Man-to-man, admittedly, was a bit strong considering Don's personality, but I didn't think Margo would think of that. "And we had several drinks while we were doing it, and it got terribly late, so I suggested that he stay over in the extra bedroom. It's as simple as that."

"Really?" She turned slightly to look up into my face. "You mean you really just spent the evening here, talking with Don?"

"Of course. Oh, we had some drinks, listened to some music, things like that." I shrugged off those other things. "What did you think I did?"

I thought...well, some body called and left a message that you were tied up on business. Only, when they said that, they giggled like it was a big joke."

I wondered briefly whether there was any legal penalty for killing a man who was already dead. "That must have been a mistake," I said, pulling her closer against me. "Maybe a bad telephone connection." I nibbled at her ear. She was losing her anger.

92

"I guess I've been a silly, jealous biddy," she said. "Will you forgive me?"

"Um hum." I ran a hand over her breasts.

"I don't know how I get into these things."

"There's something that I'd like very much to get into," I whispered, running my; hand down over her belly.

"Well, here I am," Don announced, bounding down the steps.

"So I see," I said, releasing Margo. "Look, Margo and I have got things to talk about."

"I wonder," he said, "If I oughtn't to stay. There are some things I should discuss."

"I thought you two had everything out last night," Margo said.

"Not everything," was Don's reply. "There were some interesting things that came up later."

"I'll get to them another time," I said quickly. What I most wanted now was to get him out of the apartment as soon as possible. I had not forgotten that he was under the impression that I had spent part of the night in bed with him. I didn't know just what he wanted to talk about with Margo and me, but I thought it best to postpone any such discussion.

"If that's a promise," he said, beaming, "Then I will fly along. I have millions of things I should do today, and it's so late already. Bye, now." He blew a kiss in our general direction that might have been meant for either of us, and was gone on a cloud of perfume.

Margo looked after him and sighed. "Such a sweet boy," she said, "But awfully unconventional." She turned back to me. "Now, where were we?"

I took her in my arms and pulled her close. "I was trying to get into something," I said, kissing her.

"But, darling," she murmured after a moment, "It's not even noon yet."

"I don't care," I said, patting her soft bottom, "I want what I want, and I want it now."

She laughed and wriggled against my hand. "You're such a tiger," she said. Suddenly I was everybody's tiger. I wasn't sure if the stripes were right.

I took her hand and led her toward the stairs. My hangover was far from gone, but I knew I had to do some performing if I were going to get safely back into Margo's good graces.

Upstairs in my bedroom, I set about methodically seducing her, an act that worked better if it followed certain set procedures. First, there was more necking and a great deal of feeling around. That was to put her in the mood. Then we undressed. I did not take her clothes off. She did that herself. I got them "all messed up," which she disapproved of.

At this point, the lights would ordinarily be turned off. We did not as a rule have relations in the daylight hours. In fact, this was the only such instance I could recall. This time, Margo had to be satisfied with closing the drapes, although she complained she could "still see everything."

"Close your eyes," I suggested.

"I do, but they keep coming open."

I wasn't sure whether to be flattered that my lovemaking opened her eyes, or offended that she so disliked looking at me while we were engaged in getting it on, but I knew better than to make an issue of it. Instead, having already removed my clothes, I helped her out of her underpinnings, and set about in earnest trying to prepare her for the actual deed.

I kissed her mouth. I kissed her throat. I kissed her breasts, and each taut nipple. I stroked her thighs, until I felt them part slightly, inviting me in. When she began to feel damp, it was time to kiss my way downward—bypassing the navel, she did not like that tongued—to the mound below.

I kissed her there, my tongue darting, slithering inside, and finally seeking out the little finger hidden within a soft fold of flesh. When I got there she moaned softly, opening her legs wide and pushing gently against my face.

That was the signal that everything was go. It was time to move upward into her embrace, our bodies hotly pressed together and, gently, lest she complain bout my rudeness, insert myself into her while I kissed away any lingering reservations.

Everything went according to schedule until I got to the part about entering her. There was one little difficulty at that point. I was over her and pressing against her before it oc-

94

curred to me that I didn't have a stiff dick. That is, I had a dick, all right, but it was flopping about limply.

Margo stirred impatiently and rubbed against me. "It's all right, darling," she whispered, eyes tightly closed, "You can go ahead now."

"Okay," I whispered back, rubbing more insistently against her in an effort to get it up. It remained quite soft. I reached down between us and took hold of it, trying to coax things along. Nothing.

Margo opened one eye and gave me a curious look. "Is anything wrong?" she asked.

"No, no, of course not," I assured her. I guided it to where it was supposed to go and try to force it in anyway. It was like trying to shove a wet noodle up a baby's backside. I lifted away from her and worked at it some more, with increasing desperation. Nothing happened. It was as soft as an old rubber.

"Something is wrong," Margo said, opening both eyes. She lifted her head to look down between us at my flaccid dick.

I sighed and held it up for her to see. "I'm sorry," I said, "I guess I'm just not up to it. I had a lot to drink last night."

"I wonder what else you had," she said, the ice back in her voice.

"Now, Margo, a man can't always get it up when he wants to. Things make a difference."

"What things?" she asked, squirming out from under me and getting out of bed.

"A lot of things. Like, if a guy has had too much sex...." That, of course, was not the right thing to say. "...Or if he just isn't feeling well," I added quickly. "Like me, today. I don't feel well. I think I'm coming down with something. Look." I stuck my tongue out.

"Put that away," she snapped, shimmying into her slip. "You look obscene."

The doorbell rang. "Damn," I said, "Who can that be?"

"Probably someone else to borrow your shower," she said.

I slipped into my robe and left her to finish dressing while I went downstairs. Had there been any possibility of finishing things up, I'd have ignored the door, but there wasn't. My limp friend showed not the slightest interest in getting up and about his duties. Under the circumstances, I thought any interruption was probably welcome.

"Hi," Elliot greeted me when I opened the door. He looked at my robe. "Just getting up?"

"Yes and no," I said, giving him a rueful smile. "Come on in. Look, why don't you make yourself at home? Find some coffee or a drink or something. I'll put on some clothes and join you in a minute."

"I'm not interrupting anything, am I?" he asked, hesitating in the hall.

I shook my head and sighed. "No, it was already finished.

"Don't tell me," Margo said when I came into the bathroom where she was combing her hair. "It's another buddy. He's come by to talk to you."

"As a matter of fact, yes," I said, trying to put an arm around her. She shoved my hand away. "Look, why don't we have some lunch," I said, "And maybe later…"

"I don't care to establish a time table," she said shortly. She repaired her lipstick and turned around to face me. "Honestly," she said, "It's infuriating. I'd almost swear you're cheating on me with someone else, but the only people I ever catch you with are other men. It mystifies me."

# CHAPTER TWELVE

Elliot had helped himself to some instant coffee, which he was sipping when we came downstairs. I introduced him to Margo. They didn't exactly seem to hit it off. Maybe Margo's intuition was beginning to warn her about some of those men. Maybe Elliot's super-casual manner toward her put her off. In any case, she didn't like him, and her cold politeness only underscored that face. She left after a very few minutes.

"I'll see you later," I said as I saw her out.

"Don't exhaust yourself," she said, avoiding my move to kiss her. "You must conserve your strength, after all."

I rejoined Elliot in the kitchen. "So, that's your fiancée," he said.

"Don't form an opinion on her behavior this morning," I begged. "She's not in her best state."

He shrugged and took another sip of his coffee. "Actually," he said, "I came by to apologize for that whole business yesterday. It's really no concern of mine what you do, and I had no right to spout off the way I did. There's nothing so special about my life, after all."

"Oh, I don't know, I always admired it," I said.

"Thanks. Anyway, I came by just to apologize. And to show you my heart is in the right place. I want you to come over tonight. I'm having a few friends in. It'll be like old times."

"I don't know…." I said, hesitating. I knew that I ought to spend the evening getting back in Margo's good graces, but the idea of a party at Elliot's was tempting. He had always had such interesting friends.

"Please." He assumed his tenderest expression and his voice was very coaxing. "I planned it with you in mind. Everyone wants to see you again. I promised them you would be there."

"Well, all right, if only to make an appearance," I said.

"Great." He looked genuinely delighted.

A movement behind him gave me a sudden fright. The jar of instant coffee floated out of the cupboard to the counter. A second later, a cup joined it.

"I think I'll make some coffee," I said, jumping up. I measured coffee into the cup. Something nudged me in the ribs. I took a second cup from the cupboard and measured coffee into that one too.

"I've already got a cup, thanks," Elliot said.

"That's all right," I told him nervously. "I always make an extra cup in case the first one gets cold."

I filled both cups with water from the kettle and came back to the table, seating myself so that in order to face me, Elliot would have to turn his back on the cup I had left on the counter. I had no sooner sat down that that cup lifted into the air and tilted slightly. There was a faint slurping sound.

"Did you hear something?" Elliot asked me, moving as though to turn.

"Mice," I said, putting a hand on his knee to restrain him. "Pay them no mind."

"You ought to do something about them," he said.

I shook my head and forced a smile. "Oh, no, I love mice. They're my favorite things."

"Really?" he said, surprised.

To my consternation, the cup floated over until it was directly above Elliot's head.

"I think," Elliot said, putting his own coffee down, "I'll go pee."

The cup over his head tilted threateningly. "Don't," I said without thinking.

"Don't?" He sat back into his chair with a little laugh. "Well, okay, I won't if you don't want me to, but I might have to sit with my legs crossed before too long."

98

The cup righted itself and went back to the counter. "On second thought," I said, taking Elliot's hand and pulling him up, "Maybe it would be best if you peed now."

He looked a bit bewildered. "It would be for me," he said, "Although frankly I don't know what's in it for you, unless you've taken up some peculiar habits."

When he had left the room, Lorin came into view. He yawned pointedly. "Ho, hum," he said, "I can't understand how you can turn down a cute little piece like that Don and then spend all this time with people as dull as the last two."

"In Elliot's case," I informed him, "It's because I like him, and in Margo's case, it's because I'm in love with her, as I have explained before."

"The passion seemed a little cool upstairs," he said with a smirk.

"There were reasons for that and you damn well know it. I've been going strong the last couple of days. I just wasn't up to sex today."

"Really?" He cocked an eyebrow and came closer, slipping an arm around me. I didn't try to argue the matter with him, but let him press against me and kiss me. His tongue went to work in my mouth while he squirmed against my crotch.

His mouth left mine and he giggled, and reached down to feel my cock. It had already begun to swell. "You recovered mighty fast," he said. The toilet flushed nearby. Lorin vanished before I could make a reply.

"Listen," I said to Elliot when he came back into the room., "I'm going to have a look in at the office. I'll see you tonight, okay?"

He grinned. "Sounds like I'm being run off the grounds," he said.

"Just for the moment."

He came closer and kissed me once, lightly. It was impossible not to compare it with the kiss Lorin had given me just a moment before. Lorin's had been wild, exotic, lewd. Elliot's was soft and gentle and reassuring. It made no demands, but many promises.

"Till tonight," he said, and left.

* * * * * * *

On my way to the office later, I found myself thinking about Elliot, and the affair we had been having when I met Lorin. Actually, *affair* seemed rather to overstate the case for the relationship that had existed. We had been having sex regularly, but looking back on it, I saw that that was actually the least important element. Not that the sex hadn't been enjoyable, very much so, from what I recalled, but there had been so much more that we shared.

I had almost completely forgotten the desire I'd had then to be a writer. Somewhere along the way, I had come to think of that as a hobby rather than a hoped-for career. Eventually, it had ceased to seem important even as a hobby.

In those pre-Lorin days, however, Elliot and I had lived a comfortably bohemian existence, he with his painting and I with my writing, each encouraging the other. We had dream-like plans for the future, a future, truth to tell, not much different from what had been our present. We had simple tastes in most things. We stayed home a lot, with our art. We saw a few friends, interesting, intelligent people, many of them in the arts as well. Sometimes we would go to the beach and just wander along the sand, or we would spend an afternoon staring at the masterpieces in the art museum, sharing one another's feelings without the necessity of wordy explanations.

Those memories seemed like scenes from another world, certainly from a life other than my own. All of that had changed with Lorin. It had become "wild" people, beautiful young men, giddy excitement, never a pause even to catch one's breath, let alone to reflect on life or art of beauty.

It was that existence that had left me bitter, disgusted, eager to give up the gay world, but in that Lorin period, as I thought of it, I had lost my perspective. I had forgotten that was not the whole gay scene, only a gaudy little part of it. I could understand why Elliot had been hurt and disappointed to be discarded along with Lorin's way of life as though the two were the same. I had tossed the baby with the bathwater.

Of course, one could never go back to the past. All the same, I couldn't help wondering what my life would be like now if I had gone the other way, remained with Elliot instead of going for Lorin.

It gave me an uncomfortable feeling to realize that my absence from the office seemed to have mattered not at all. I stared at the small stack of trivial memos my secretary brought me and tried to think what really important responsibilities I had about the place, but the fact was, there was almost nothing I did that Miss Byrd couldn't attend to quite efficiently herself.

Of course, I took part in shaping company policy. I suggested all sorts of things to Mr. Sellers, Margo's father, and Mr. Sellers, her uncle. I attended all sorts of meeting, although, in fact, I frequently spent the time daydreaming.

I decided I was being unfair to myself. An executive's value wasn't measured in the amount of paperwork he put out. Probably if one examined the actual workload of the other men around the place, the ones at my level of management, it might seem as if they, too, did nothing to justify their places here. The only difference was that Lorin had been putting ideas into my head. Nothing had actually changed since last week, and I had been happy enough then. I closed my eyes and tried to remember how happy I had been last week—but the memory failed to come.

I scribbled some notes at the bottom of one of the sheets of paper on my desk and summoned Miss Byrd to my office. "Put this into a letter," I said, handing her the paper.

"Very good, sir," she said, giving me one of her odd smiles. When she smiled, Miss Byrd's mouth assumed a round shape. Indeed, Miss Byrd was a round person. I had not, in more than a year of working together, been able to find a truly straight line to her body. Everything curved, from her little moon-face to her round boobs, to her round and not-so-little bottom as she wriggled toward the door. I thought, as I had many times, that her ass was shaped like a target, just waiting for me to take aim.

Someone else thought so too apparently. I heard the twang of a rubber band and caught a glimpse of a paper clip shooting through the air to land with a ping on one of those jelly-like cheeks. Miss Byrd whirled about, her eyes round.

"Mr. Ross," was all she could say, but she fled without waiting for a reply, looking anxiously over her round shoulder as she closed the door roundly.

"Why did you do that?" I asked resignedly when Lorin appeared.

He sat on the corner of my desk, in his customary state of undress. "Do you mean to tell me it never crossed your mind?" he asked.

"I don't do all the things that cross my mind," I said.

"Pity. You should try it for a change. It makes one feel so much better."

"I feel quite well enough, thank you. Or did," I corrected myself, "Before you came back on the scene."

"Are you sorry I came back, darling?" he asked, suddenly serious.

"Yes," I grumbled.

"Really and truly? I know you've fussed a lot. You always did. But you did love me, once, and the other night, when we had sex, you seemed to enjoy it."

"Of course I enjoyed it," I admitted begrudgingly, "But, dammit...."

He had stood, and now he came to me, not as a coquette, but with that coaxing look of his that had never failed to melt my resolve. Despite my vows to remain cool to him, I took him in my arms and returned the kiss he gave me.

I was not immediately aware that he had vanished. I suppose I should be grateful that he at least heard Mr. Sellers open the door, but it did leave me in a rather silly pose, with my arms encircling what appeared to be nothing but air, mouth stretched out of shape, and tongue extended.

I heard a sharp intake of breath and looked around to see Margo's father staring at me in a most peculiar manner.

"Oh, Mr. Sellers," I said, dropping my arms to my sides. "I didn't hear you come in."

"I thought not," he said, clearing his throat. Several of his chins wobbled. "If it's not being too personal, would you mind telling me what on earth you were doing?"

"I was...exercising," I said in a burst of inspiration. "Yes. It's a new facial exercise, you see, sort of a combination of isometrics and Zen Buddhism. You pucker your mouth up, just as if you were kissing somebody, see." I screwed my mouth up.

"You had your arms out in front of you," he said.

"It's just that I find it hard to pretend I'm kissing someone unless I also pretend I'm embracing them." I put my arms up again.

"I see," he said, in a voice that said he did not see at all. Mr. Sellers was a big man with a small mind. "I wonder if you'd mind discontinuing your, uh, exercise for the moment. It's rather disconcerting."

I dropped my arms and put my face back into shape. "Yes, sir. Was there something you wanted to talk to me about? Maybe something that came up in my absence that requires my personal attention?"

"I can't imagine what that could be," he said. "As a matter of fact, all I wanted was to ask you if you and Margo couldn't come out to the ranch over next weekend. Mrs. Sellers and I will be going out Friday night and we thought we'd have a few people in Saturday."

"Why, yes, I'd love to. I'll check with Margo and...."

"She's agreeable," he said. "I just wanted to clear it with you."

"I see." I had the impression that attendance came close to being obligatory and that asking me and my accepting were only token gestures.

"Fine. I'll see you then, if not before." He started from the room, then paused and turned back. "Everything is all right, isn't it? Between the two of you, I mean?"

"With Margo and me? Yes, of course, everything is just fine. What makes you ask?"

"Nothing. Just make sure it stays that ways." He turned again to go. There was a faint twang and another paper clip hit its mark.

"Ow!" Mr. Sellers clapped a hand over his generous posterior and looked angrily back at me.

"What's wrong?" I asked with all the innocence I could muster.

"Something hit me," he said.

"Hit you?" I looked wildly about the room. "I can't imagine...oh, wait, yes, I know. It was a bee, I'll bet. There

103

was one in here a minute ago, buzzing around. You know, buzz, buzz, buzz...." I did the best imitation I could of a buzzing bee.

"It felt like a paper clip," he said, eyeing me speculatively.

"A paper clip? Now, really, Mr. Sellers, what would a bee being doing with a paper clip? Doesn't make much sense, does it?"

"I suppose not," he agreed. He went on his way, rubbing his butt gingerly.

# CHAPTER THIRTEEN

Elliot's party was in full swing when I arrived a little after nine. I had already spent nearly an hour arguing with Lorin, who anticipated a deadly affair.

"You should feel right at home then," I told him, which earned me several choice replies.

Actually, it was not Elliot's typical sort of party. In the past, "party" coming from Elliot meant a few close, intelligent friends in for drinks and some quiet conversation, something that I had always enjoyed before Lorin entered the picture.

Tonight's affair, however, was definitely a bash. The music could be heard a couple of blocks away. All the lights were on, the doors open, and the studio was crowded with milling people of every description.

"Now this," Lorin whispered into my ear, "Is more like it."

"You stay out of sight," I ordered.

"I will not. In this mob, who'll notice a dead lady?"

There was no sign of Elliot, but with the crowd on hand he could have been just a few feet away and still stay out of sight. I decided the logical first step was to get myself a drink.

"Which way is the liquor?" I asked a tall, gaunt woman in a fur that looked to be made of a chenille bathmat and mascara.

"Straight ahead," she said in a baritone voice, pointing toward the opposite corner of the studio. She thrust a glass toward me. "Bring me a banana sidecar while you're at it, please, sweets."

I took her glass and began pushing my way through the crowd. When somebody squealed and glowered, I remembered that an invisible Lorin was close at hand. Not wanting to get blamed for all of his mischief, I put my hands over my head, in plain view. Conversation floated by in little snatches.

"...So she said, Mary—she always calls me Mary for short, to dispense with me—she says, Mary, where will I wear the corsage? So I says to her, why not wear it up your ass, Louise, you've had everything else up there, including my flashlight."

"...High assed number. Honestly, an ass like a shelf, you could have served a buffet off it...."

"...A body like Joan Crawford, mile wide shoulders and no ass at all...."

"...And he said that this number said that he should be in movies with his looks. Well, all I can say is, I thought animal films were out of fashion...."

"His wife, can you imagine that, having the nerve to show up at my door, saying she could do anything for him I could, and I asked her if she had ever tried to fuck him in the ass.

"If you ever have children, I want the pick of the litter."

I reached the bar finally and ordered a scotch and soda from the tired-looking queen standing there. Lorin nudged me and whispered, "I'll have the same."

"Make that two," I said.

When they came, Lorin took one out of my hand and strolled casually away. I watched for a moment, but no one in the packed apartment seemed to pay any attention to the glass floating around by itself, so I shrugged and decided I needn't worry either.

Elliot found me a few minutes later. "Hi," he greeted me, putting an arm around me in a welcoming hug. "Saw you a little while ago, but it's taken this long just to get across the room."

"I don't remember you giving this kind of party," I said, practically shouting to be heard over the din.

"I don't as a rule. I thought you might enjoy it more. It's the kind of thing you and Lorin used to do."

106

"I'm not sure that's a great recommendation," I said, "But thanks anyway."

"I'm only number two," he said. "I have to try harder."

We were separated for a moment. When we got back together, Elliot said, "I keep looking around because I got reports of a naked guest somewhere in the room."

"Male guest?" I asked, guessing at once who it was.

"So I hear. Have you seen anyone like that since you got here?"

"No." It was the truth. Lorin had been invisible when he was beside me.

Elliot stretched a little taller and looked slowly around the room. "Well, I don't see hide nor hair of him. If he's here, he must just disappear at will."

"That's possible," I said.

He laughed. A half empty glass of scotch and soda drifted by behind him and a voice that he might have recognized if he had been listening more closely mumbled, "Excuse me."

"I'd better check on the bar supplies," Elliot said. "Don't go away. I'll be back in a while."

He had scarcely drifted away when I heard another familiar voice close at hand. "Hi," Don Clayton said, touching my shoulder.

I turned toward him with surprise. "I didn't expect to see you here," I said. "I didn't even know you knew Elliot."

"I don't," he said with a grin. "Is that the hostess's name?"

"Better say host when he's within hearing range," I said. "But how did you get invited if you don't know him?"

"It was kind of strange, actually. I got this anonymous phone call from someone who said he was an old friend. He said there was going to be this fabulous party and why didn't I just come on over. So, here I am."

"But you don't know who your caller was?"

"No. I thought at first it might be you, but I decided it wasn't your voice. It did sound familiar, though. I guess he'll show himself before the night's over."

"Probably," I agreed. I was pretty sure who his mysterious friend was, and evidently Lorin was already showing himself—all of himself—from time to time.

"Let's dance," Don said. He had been swaying his hips in time to the insistent bet of the music blaring through the apartment.

"I'm not very good at that kind of dancing," I said a bit apologetically.

"Oh, sure you are," he said. "Anyone who can move the way you do in bed can do these dances."

He took my drink and set it on a nearby table. "Do this," he said, and began to shuffle his feet and toss his head. I tried, feeling spastic.

"No, no, not like that," he said. "Let the beat go all the way through. Here and here." He put his hands on my hips and guided me. I watched his feet for a minute and followed his example.

"That's better. Now the shoulders, the head, the arms. That's it. Get everything going at once."

Strangely, it began to feel less silly and more fun. I actually was beginning to feel the music coursing through me. There was something strangely relaxing about the strenuous gyrations.

"Fabulous," Don said, grinning at me. "Try this." He demonstrated a fresh twist. I more or less duplicated it.

"Not bad," he said. "You're pretty wild actually."

"I'm beginning to feel that way." I tried what looked like a simple spin when done by a couple near us. My feet got twisted and I sat hard on the floor instead.

"It isn't funny," I said, getting up and glowering at a laughing Don'

"Yes it is," he said. "Come on, try again."

"Wait a minute." I was also learning that dancing like this in a jam-packed space gave one a hell of a thirst. I retrieved my drink and emptied it. A fresh one suddenly appeared before me. "Thanks," I murmured and took a long swallow.

"Where did that drink come from?" Don asked, looking about curiously.

"Beats me," I said with a giggle. "Straight from heaven, probably."

We danced some more. By this time I was getting pretty damned good. At least, I felt that I was getting pretty good, and I had learned that with this type of dancing, how you feel yourself is the important thing. Even your partner is superfluous, although it was difficult to think of anyone as pretty as Don being superfluous.

"I have to go powder my nose," Don said after a while, and disappeared into the crowd. He was hardly gone when Lorin appeared before me. Fortunately, he had donned a pair of slacks, but nothing else.

"You got dressed," I said. "What's the occasion?"

"I wanted to dance with you," he said. "We haven't done that in years."

"I might say there's a good reason," I said. "Anyway, this is not the kind of music we used to dance to."

"Oh, I put some other records on," he said. He snapped his fingers. There was the harsh sound of a needle scraping across the surface of an L.P., the records changed, and we were suddenly listening to the soft, sentimental strains of an old Sinatra ballad: Strangers in the Night.

"More tricks," I said grumpily, taking him into my arms.

"There's nothing wrong with tricks," he said. "Good tricks, anyway. Now don't be a fussbudget. You used to love dancing, remember?"

"Yes. Only nobody dances this way anymore."

"Their loss."

"I don't know," I said, swaying dreamily with him. "I was beginning to enjoy that other stuff. It's sort of wild and free feeling. Out of sight, to use the modern idiom."

"I know all about being out of sight."

We were the only couple dancing at the moment. Apparently no one else appreciated Lorin's choice of music. In fact, they attempted to change it back. The slow, romantic Sinatra song vanished as suddenly as it had started and the loud, raucous beat was back again.

But only for a moment. Lorin glowered and snapped his fingers. Again there was that awful scraping, the clunk of a record changing, and our ballad was back.

"That's hard on somebody's records," I said, taking up the dancing where we had left off. The truth was, though, that I didn't mind. I did enjoy the old-fashioned music and the old-fashioned dancing, and I'd had more than enough to drink to put me in a romantic mood. I held Lorin closer and closed my eyes to do a neat turn and a dip.

"Boy, do you look silly," Don said close by. I opened my eyes, startled. Lorin, who must have seen Don coming, had neatly disappeared, leaving me dancing quite by myself.

"I was just practicing while I waited for you," I said quickly, holding my arms open for him.

"Well, I don't do the minuet," he said. "What happened to the real music?"

As if on cue, the music started up again, louder than before. Someone apparently thought to scare away the evil jinx with loud noise.

"That's more like it," Don said, beginning to gyrate again.

"You know," I said, "This could prove to be quite a night."

Elliot came by a minute later, bringing me a fresh drink. Don seemed not to notice that we had been joined, and for a minute I continued dancing while I talked to Elliot.

"For God's sake, quit that jumping around while I'm talking to you," Elliot said. "It makes me dizzy."

"Sorry," I said, standing still. Don kept right on dancing. I wasn't sure he even noticed that I had stopped. He was already more than a little drunk, and I was right there with him.

"I think maybe I had better warn you," Elliot said. "I just had an alarming experience. There's a guy here tonight who looks like Lorin's twin brother."

"That's strange, isn't it," I said uneasily. "Did he mention what his name is?"

"No, I didn't talk to him, as a matter of fact. I just saw him at a distance, but when I got to where he had been, he was gone."

"Maybe it was the distance," I said, "Or the liquor."

"They probably helped, but even allowing for that, he sure was a look-alike."

110

"Maybe it was Lorin," I said with a laugh. "It would be just like him, you know."

He laughed too. "Seriously, though," he said, "I just wanted to warn you before you ran into him and thought you were seeing ghosts. Of course, Lorin would be older now. He didn't have a younger brother, by any chance, did he?"

"I don't think Lorin even had a mother and father," I said, "And certainly no brothers."

"Born from sea foam?" he asked with a twinkle in his eye.

"That was Aphrodite. If Lorin is like one of the love deities, I'd nominate Eros. He was in charge of the earthy, physical pleasures. But as far as his manner of birth, I'd be more inclined to expect something like Minerva. If you recall, Jupiter had a headache and had his wife take an axe to his head, and lo and behold, out jumped Minerva, dressed for battle and full grown."

"Hell of a cure for a headache," Elliot said.

"I guess the only one who really liked the whole business was Minerva," I said.

"Minerva who?" Don asked. He had finally discovered that I was no longer dancing with him, to use the phrase loosely, and had come to investigate.

"Some old dyke," I said. I doubted that mythology would be of interest to Don. "Have you met your host? Elliot, Don."

"How do you do?" Elliot said, looking him up and down as they shook hands.

"Pleased to have the honor of meeting your acquaintance," 'Don said, making a drunken attempt at a curtsey.

Elliot blinked and said, "I guess so."

Someone called to Elliot just then from across the room. "Excuse me," he said to me, and with a nod in Don's direction, he began to push his way in the direction of the voice.

"I just met Lorin," Don said.

I nearly choked on the liquor in my mouth. "You just what?" I sputtered.

"I met Lorin," he said with an air of complete innocence and nonchalance.

"Lorin who?" There was always an outside chance that I was being overly jumpy. After all, my Lorin—my ex-Lorin—was not the only Lorin in the world.

"Your ex," he said.

"Do you know what you're saying?"

"What kind of a silly question is that," he asked. "Of course I know what I'm saying. I'm not stupid, you know. I said I just met Lorin Gebhard, your ex-boyfriend."

"That isn't possible," I said. "Lorin is dead."

He shook his head stubbornly. "That what I thought, but he certainly isn't. I just met him and talked to him. He pinched my ass, as a matter of fact."

"Maybe it's a mistake," I suggested without much confidence. "Maybe it's somebody who just looks like Lorin. That happens, you know. It happens all the time."

He shook his head again. "It was Lorin. I said to him, 'Aren't you Lorin?' and he said, 'Yes, I am.' So it couldn't be a mistake, could it?"

"It has to be some kind of mistake, doesn't it," I argued.

He shrugged and gave his head a toss. "Beats me, but he's alive now, and well."

I glanced around apprehensively. In the distance I saw Elliot working his way toward us. I did not want him joining in this conversation.

"Look," I said, taking Don's arm firmly. "It's too crowded here. Let's you and I go some place less busy, all right?"

"Like where?" he asked, resisting.

"Like my apartment."

"I don't want to go yet," he said, pouting. "Parties aren't really fun until very, very late, when the boring people have given up and gone home."

"Then let's go somewhere and come back later," I said, feeling trapped.

"We might not get back in. Sometimes when a party gets late and starts swinging, they lock the doors. I've been to lots of parties where that's happened. Of course, I was always inside when they locked the doors. I never got locked out."

"That won't happen here," I argued, tugging at his arm. "Elliot never locks his door, honest. He never even closes it. It stands open day and night, winter and summer."

"I'll bet we could find a bedroom right here in this apartment," he said, looking around. "Then we wouldn't even have to leave at all, and we'd be here in case things get hot later."

"I think they're hot enough already," I said, practically yanking him off his feet. I pretended I didn't even see Elliot wave. I knew where the bedroom was, and with all the people milling about, Elliot wasn't too likely to see where we went.

I started breathing again when the bedroom door closed behind us. All I had to do was keep out of sight until I could…actually, I didn't know what I meant to do, but until I did know, I wanted to keep Don out of circulation, and I knew only one way of doing that.

*THE GAY HAUNT*, BY VICTOR J. BANIS

# CHAPTER FOURTEEN

"My, you are the hot one," Don said when I released him from a long, torrid kiss.

"You ain't seen nothing yet," I warned him. "Let's get out of these clothes, okay?"

He cast a glance in the direction of the door. :"Maybe we ought to leave the clothes on, in case anyone comes in. That could be embarrassing. I wouldn't want anyone to think I came here just to trick."

I flipped the lock on the door. "There, no intruders, okay?"

"Well…." He still looked a little hesitant. I came back to where he was standing and kissed him again, full force, running my hands over the full little mounds of his backside. That, apparently, was where the switch was hidden. "All right," he said brightly, wriggling against me.

I gave his butt a smack. "Out of the clothes," I said. Naked, I felt I had a better chance of keeping him here. Lorin was one of the few people I had known who went around crowded rooms naked. I was hoping Don was a little more modest.

I was already undressed by the time he had shed his briefs. He looked quite delectable, in fact, so the effort I was making was not merely a precaution. As for my fears about taking Margo's cousin to bed, they no longer seemed valid, since he thought we had done it already.

We kissed again, and I fell backward, taking him with me to the bed. I rolled him over and inserted a tongue in his ear, making him squeal. His naked flesh felt like velvet to my roaming hands. This was altogether a pleasant task I had set myself.

We rolled onto our sides, facing one another. He pulled slightly away from me and slid downward, working his way down to my crotch. My cock was certainly more than ready for him by the time he got there. I gasped with excitement as he clasped it and brought his mouth to the head. The lips slipped warmly over it and he sucked it deep into his throat.

I scrambled around on the bed, careful not to interfere with what he was doing, and managed to get into a sixty-nine position. His own cock tasted sweet and young and altogether delicious. I sucked on it hungrily, my nose buried in his balls. I had a splendid view of his ass, with its dimpled cheeks and the soft inviting valley between. I cupped my hands over the soft mounds, massaging them lightly. He pushed back gently against my hands.

I pressed him forward slightly, rolling over again until he was above me and I was on my back. I licked at his dangling balls and began to work my way beyond, pulling his cheeks gently apart as I licked my way upward. My tongue reached the core and he sighed happily and pushed back against my face.

I slid back, between his legs, and got to my knees behind him. It was just too good not to crawl into. I didn't need any lubricant, either. The spit he had left on my dick and the spit I had left on his hole were all that was necessary. I brought the head to the opening and worked it carefully in. He bent further, lifting his ass up, to make the entry easier for me. He was hot and tight, clinging to my rod as I thrust in. I paused, waiting until I felt the muscles relax slightly, then going a little deeper.

"Oh, give it to me," he murmured, wriggling his ass slightly.

I did. I drove it home, filling his ass with eager cock. He welcomed it greedily, groaning with pleasure as he pushed back on it. It went in to the hilt, the entire shaft disappearing as his ass brushed my balls. It was sheer heaven! No wonder Lorin had had such a pleasant time.

Fucking Don, however, got progressively wilder. I was somewhat akin to riding a bucking bronco. He was certainly not the sort to just sit or kneel there while you poked. He began to swing his hips, gyrating them much as he had done

116

when we were dancing. My thrusts were almost unnecessary. He bounced and bobbed and twisted and writhed, and my cock kept feeling harder and bigger and hotter until it was close to exploding. We were both sweating, our bodies making little slapping sounds as they came together.

It was not long before I felt that familiar, delightful ache in my balls. Deep down inside me a knot of tension began to grow. It swelled, seeming to fill me entirely, and then it was rushing down and out, erupting into the hot receptacle of his ass, and I was clinging fiercely to him, groaning and gasping for breath.

It took several long seconds to regain my senses. Finally, reluctantly, I slid my prick from the still-tight opening. I pushed him down on the bed and reached for his cock. It felt wet and sticky to my grasp.

"I'll bring you off," I said, lowering my head toward him.

"Not necessary," he whispered.

"Of course it is. Fair is fair."

"Not necessary," he repeated. "I already came. While you were fucking me."

I felt more carefully. He wasn't kidding. I had heard of guys who got so excited getting fucked that they shot without anything more being needed, but this was the first time it had ever happened with me. With Lorin, a little hand action had been employed if we wanted to come together.

"Well, I'll be damned," I said. I fell back on the bed and gave his ass a pat. "You're pretty good."

"So are you," he said. After a pause, he added, "You know, I wish Lorin had been with us. I've never had a three-way, but with you and him I know it would be fun."

I sat up on the bed. "Look, about this Lorin business," I said, measuring my words carefully. "I think you had better forget all about what you told me."

"What's that?" he asked.

"About seeing Lorin. People will think you were drunk, if they're kind, or maybe even crazy."

"Why?" he wanted to know.

"Because," I said again, "Lorin is dead. He is six feet under the ground."

"Pish posh," Lorin said, popping into view. "I may be three sheets to the wind, but that's all."

"You see," Don said, giving me a triumphant look. "I told you." He seemed quite unperturbed by Lorin's unusual manner of entrance.

"I thought we had an agreement..." I said angrily to Lorin.

"He's already seen me tonight," Lorin interrupted. "So it seems pointless to keep hiding from him. Anyway, we met before."

"Five years ago," Don said.

"More recently than that," Lorin said. "At Paul's. That was me in bed with you."

"You?" Don's eyes widened in surprise. He looked at me, then Lorin, and back to me. "Well, isn't that funny? I was wondering why your cock wasn't as big."

"I didn't hear you complaining," I said, vaguely offended. I couldn't see any necessity for telling him all this.

"He's been telling everyone you were dead," Don said to Lorin.

"Well, I am, sort of," Lorin said. "But it's really all very complicated and I don't know that anything is going to be accomplished by going into it. Why don't we just agree that this will be a secret between the three of us, and that will be that?"

"Sure thing," Don said brightly. "As long as a guy is groovy and good in bed, what do I care about his background or where he comes from?"

"That's the spirit," Lorin said. He turned on me, obviously intending to charm me into a better humor. "See, everything is fine."

"I'm not sure." I leaned a little closer and peered at him. "You're drunk. I didn't think ghosts got that way."

"No law against it. And you're a fine one to talk."

He was right, I was squiffed too, and feeling it more than ever, having burned off a little energy with Don. "I suppose we should have some coffee," I said.

"Like hell," Lorin replied. "I've worked too hard to get this way. Honestly, every time I'd get a drink mixed, somebody would come along and take it right out of my hand.

118

"Besides," Don chimed in, "Why go to all the trouble of getting that way just to not be?" He frowned as a new thought crossed what, for want of a better description, could be termed his mind. "Only, what will we have to drink? There's nothing in here."

Lorin gave a wave of his hand. "There is now," he said. A magnum of champagne and three glasses appeared on the dresser.

"I thought you waved wands to do that sort of thing," I said. "Or is that the fairy drag-mothers?"

"If I waved my wand, it would come," Lorin said. "I haven't had anything tonight, and I got awfully horny watching you two."

"That's no problem," Don said quickly.

"A child after my own heart," Lorin said.

"It's not year heart he's after," I suggested.

"But first," Lorin said, ignoring my comment, "A glass of bubbly." He poured the sparkling liquid into the three glasses and handed them around. I figured, what the hell, and emptied my glass. Lorin filled it again almost at once.

"Gee," Don said, sighing happily and looking from one to the other of us. "All we need now is a roaring fire in the fireplace."

"That's very simple," Lorin said, weaving a little unsteadily. He was obviously having a grand time showing off. Of course, I had not been very appreciative of these stunts of his since he came back, so it was logical he would delight in having a better audience. "Fire is something of a specialty where I come from."

He waved his hand again without even looking from the champagne he was pouring. A warm blaze appeared at the wall behind him. I emptied my glass again and lay back on the bed. Sometimes it's wisest not to argue with the fates. I couldn't at the moment rid myself of either of them, so I might as well relax and enjoy them.

"To love," Lorin said in the way of a toast, lifting his glass in what I considered a rather flashy gesture.

Don lifted his in return. "I never met a man I didn't love," he said, finishing off the sparkling liquid in one fell swoop.

Lorin came closer and filled my glass again. I tried and confirmed that one cannot drink lying down. I sat up and lifted the glass to my lips.

I didn't drink, however. The flicker of flames beyond Lorin caught my attention. My first thought was that Elliot had one huge fireplace in his bedroom.

Then I remembered what should have occurred to me before—Elliot didn't have a fireplace in his bedroom. And Lorin hadn't thought to conjure one up to go with the fire.

As a result, half the room was now ablaze.

# CHAPTER FIFTEEN

"Lorin," I cried, pointing.

He turned and saw the fire. "Oh, for heaven's sake, what happened there?"

"It's that damned fire you started," I said. "There was no fireplace there."

"Never occurred to me," Lorin said, looking thoughtfully at the flames licking up to the ceiling.

"Well, don't just stand there staring," I cried. "Put the damned thing out!"

"I don't know how," he said.

"What?"

"Where I come from, we learn to start them. There's never any reason to extinguish them."

The noises of the party, which I had thought were getting unusually loud, were a roar now, and I realized that the fire was the general topic of discussion. Somewhere in the distance, but growing louder, I recognized the sound of a fire siren.

"Where are our clothes?" I asked gruffly, getting off the bed.

"I put them all on the chair," Don said.

"I don't see any chair," I said, looking around.

"It was over there," Don explained, pointing to where the fire burned brightest.

"I don't know why you're worrying about clothes," Lorin said. "It seems plenty warm in here. I was glad to get rid of mine."

He was naked again by this time. That, however, was not much of a consolation. The fire was on the wall that held the door out of the bedroom—no escape by that route.

121

"You realize," I said, "That we could be burned alive."

"In my case," Lorin said, "That would be difficult."

"Don and I could end up joining you," I said.

"That wouldn't be so bad," Lorin said, screwing up his face thoughtfully. "I mean, we do make an attractive three-some, don't you agree, and we could have such fun."

"Lorin!" I snapped.

"Oh, all right, if you're going to be fussy about it." He looked annoyed. "There's a window over there, and a fire escape outside."

"I don't suppose you could produce some clothes for us, could you?" I asked. The closet was unreachable by this time, and the bedroom was now like an inferno, but I was nonetheless a little reluctant to go running out dressed as we were—or, undressed, as the case were.

"I think you both look lovely," Lorin said.

"God damn it, I don't feel lovely," I said, not caring if I hurt his feelings. The fire was inching toward my feet. "Get me some clothes, right now, or I'll report you as a failure as a spirit."

"All right, all right, don't get your bowels in an uproar. Honestly." He made a movement of his hand and stamped his foot twice. There was suddenly a beaded evening gown on the bed before me.

"What in the name of heaven is this?" I demanded, holding it up for inspection. It looked like a Salvation Army reject. Hell, it looked like a Drag Ball reject.

"You were in such a hurry, I didn't take time to shop around," Lorin explained.

"I think it's gorgeous," Don said, taking it and fingering the material.

"You wear it then," I said, yanking a blanket off the bed and wrapping it around me. The window was stuck. I had to take one of the pillows to it and knock the glass out.

"Careful," I warned the others, climbing through with my blanket tucked about my legs.

Don had actually taken time to put on the gown. It looked more than a little weird. Even if it had been a lovely gown, and he a qualified drag queen, it would have looked strange without wig, makeup, shoes, or any such garnishes.

122

"You really aren't going down on the street with that on?" I asked.

"It's chilly out here," he said, lifting his skirt to climb over the windowsill.

The fire escape was over an alley. Below, we could see a part of the street, a beehive of activity. Red lights flashed on and off, sirens still wailed, and over it all was the hubbub of countless voices. I felt more than a little silly in a blanket, accompanied by one naked man and another in a beaded gown, but the only alternative was remaining where we were, which could mean being burnt to a crisp.

"Let's go," I muttered, starting down. Don followed close at my heels, taking pains not to trip over his skirt, and Lorin trailed, seemingly in no particular hurry, although of course he was in no particular danger, either. Being dead has its advantages, that was plain.

I had hoped we might escape detection, but there was just too much going on below, and too many people—and we were a conspicuous trio, to say the least. Fortunately, Lorin remained behind me, so that, surprisingly enough, Don and I got most of the attention.

Perhaps the greatest irony of all was that by the time we got to the street, sticking as close to the walls as possible for shelter, most of the excitement was over.

"It's all under control," one woman assured me. "Fire's practically out. They're looking for the damage now."

I was wondering if we couldn't possibly go back up the fire escape and avoid the embarrassment of a frontal entrance, when Lorin gave my blanket a tug.

"Look," he said, pointing.

I looked, but saw nothing unusual. Nothing unusual, that is to say, at the site of a fire. There were crowds, mostly staring in the other direction, and a hook and ladder track parked at the curb, apparently not needed.

"I don't see anything but a fire truck," I said.

"That's it," he said. "I've always wanted to drive one. I didn't dare before, I was afraid I'd get killed, but now I don't have to worry. Come on, let's go for a ride."

"Are you crazy?" I asked, staring wide-eyed. "Maybe you can't get killed, but I can."

"Oh, what's wrong with you, Paul, always nit-picking?" He was already headed toward the truck. "I'm going for a ride. Anyone who wants to join me, climb aboard. Don, how about you?"

"It sounds scary," he said. A smile flitted across his features. "But it sounds like fun, too. Wait for me."

Everyone, of course, was paying attention to the apartment building and the firemen scurrying in and out the front door. No one noticed Lorin, naked as a jaybird, helping Don, in his beaded gown, onto the truck.

"You can't drive this thing alone," I yelled. "It takes two people to drive one of these jobs, one up front, and one back here."

"What are you standing there for, then?" Lorin yelled back, already at the wheel. He waved his hand and I was suddenly *sans* blanket. I threw a hand over my cock and looked around for someplace to hide. The rear of the truck was the nearest place. I made a jump for it just as it started to roll.

Someone shouted and I blinked. I suppose I had thought somebody might manage to stop Lorin, or perhaps he was only kidding, or perhaps he might not even know how to get it started, but before I could even reconsider and jump off, the siren suddenly split the air and we roared away with more speed than I would have thought the mammoth machine capable of.

"Lorin!" I shouted at the top of my lungs, clinging frantically to a handle of some sort or other and aware that, bare-assed, I was not only conspicuous but a damn good target if anyone decided to shoot—which, unfortunately, I considered a good possibility.

He shouted something back. It sounded like, "Steer the back end!" We flew down the street, siren screaming. For the moment, he was all right, although the rear end was weaving back and forth dangerously, but he would never get this beast around a corner without some help back here, and if he piled up now, I had more to lose than he did. I swallowed and scrambled up to the seat and the extra wheel positioned back there to take care of the wide swinging rear.

In his own way, Lorin could be quite thoughtful. A big tumbler of champagne suddenly appeared on a tray before me. I took the glass and the tray disappeared. The champagne helped with the fluttering in my stomach. I didn't mind at all when it refilled itself.

Ahead of me, I could see Lorin's naked back. Don was standing and hanging out one side, silvery gown fluttering behind him.

Behind us, there was a considerable uproar. People had shouted as we sped away, but by now there were other sirens and red lights roaring away from the curb in hot pursuit.

"Lorin," I screamed, not at all sure he could even hear me over the din, "They're after us. They'll arrest us. I'll go to prison."

He decided, apparently, that they would have to catch us first. I tried to sit down, but the combination of cool night air and leather did not make the seat comfortable. I jumped up when my balls touched the cold seat, and sent the back end of the truck sweeping wide to the left.

"Easy," I told myself, bringing it back into line. I wondered helplessly if there were some way of stopping my half without bothering the front end, but I wasn't sure enough to risk anything.

We were suddenly taking a corner. I put all the muscle I could into the huge wheel before me. Somehow the rear end managed to get around the corner as well. I was so engrossed in that maneuver that it was a moment or so before I realized that we were on the Sunset Strip. Of course, with the sirens and lights going, the traffic was no problem, but the Strip was always crowded, with everything from hippies to Midwest tourists. And even in that exotic scene, we were a striking sight, two of us naked and one more or less in drag. Lorin was brandishing a champagne glass as though blessing the crowds. Someone cheered and I toasted him with my glass as we swept past. I tried keeping a hand over my crotch, but found that impossible without spilling my champagne, which I considered increasingly important.

I looked over my shoulder. The police and fire vehicles were a veritable parade in hot pursuit, and gaining rapidly on us. I tried shouting at Lorin and signaling, but he had chosen to ignore me for a time, basking as he was in the glow of considerable attention, which had always delighted him.

He suddenly gave me a signal for another turn, and almost before I knew what was happening, we screeched around another corner, the rear end swinging wide as I fought to keep it under some kind of control. I hadn't even begun to establish any such control when Lorin took us around yet another corner, this one looking altogether too small for the truck to fit into. It was an alley, in fact. I realized he was trying to dodge our pursuers, although the idea of hiding a multi-ton fire truck in an alley seemed rather farfetched to my way of thinking.

Of course, I had reckoned without Lorin's talents, those that he had acquired in the last five years. I looked back to see that the entrance to the alley was now a solid wall of rose bushes and trellises, hiding us from view. Sirens shrieked and lights flashed through the growth as the chasing vehicles raced by.

I let out the breath I had been holding—as nearly as I could calculate, since we left the apartment building. Lorin was already scrambling down from the front end.

"Better move," he yelled, "They'll be back in a minute."

"Where would you suggest we go?" I called back. "I'm going to look a little conspicuous on the Strip."

"Move up in the world," he called. He worked the appropriate switches to send the huge ladder suddenly climbing upward.

"I will not," I said. I had no intention of perching atop a ladder until discovered by the police, and unless I wanted to break into one of the apartments in the building before me, I couldn't see that the ladder was going to take me anywhere.

The sirens were suddenly growing louder again. The police were coming back. Lorin was right, or course, it hadn't taken them any time at all to discover that the fire truck that they had been chasing had disappeared. In a minute or so they would surely discover the hidden alley.

I glanced back to where Lorin had been, but he had Don had disappeared. I looked around frantically. One side of the alley was a high wall which I had no chance of getting over and which apparently only bordered a parking lot anyway.

126

The other side of the alley was a line of apartment buildings. I ran to the one nearest me, trying a door that apparently led to laundry facilities. It was locked.

Up seemed the logical direction after all. Maybe I could find an empty apartment and borrow some clothes. Without clothes, it mattered little which way I went. I was bound to stand out like a sore thumb.

I looked up. One window on the fourth floor was open and dark. That seemed to offer the best possibilities. I guided the ladder as close to it as I was able in my inexperience and began to climb hastily upward.

I made it none too soon. I had just reached the ledge outside the open window when a police car stopped at the end of the alley. I balanced on the ledge and gave the ladder a shove—no use leaving too obvious a trail. Then I hoisted myself up to the high sill and wriggled through the open window.

The room inside was pitch dark. I could only guess how far the floor was, and what might be on it, but I damn well couldn't stay where I was. I took a deep breath and dropped through—and landed, not on the floor, but on a bed.

The bed was occupied. I found myself suddenly amidst a profusion of flesh.

*THE GAY HAUNT*, BY VICTOR J. BANIS

# CHAPTER SIXTEEN

"My God," a male voice said from beneath me. "We're caught. It's my wife!"

"Your wife?" a female voice said. "I didn't know you had a wife!"

"I beg your pardon," I said, trying to extricate myself from the tangle of arms and legs. "But I'm not your wife, sir."

A hand felt along my leg, reached my cock, and grasped it. "You're right," the woman said. "He's not your wife, Henry." The hand stayed where it was, however, stroking with what seemed like more than casual interest. My own hand was imprisoned under an ample derriere. I squeezed, and the ass squirmed a little

"Who are you, then?" the man demanded.

"No one you know," I said. "I was just passing by and thought I'd drop in." I felt along the curve of the ass to the thighs, and between the legs. What I found was rather puny. I could see why the woman had left her hand where it was.

"Not now, Doris," the man said. "I want to get to the bottom of things."

I had already accomplished that myself. My foot was resting against another thigh. Presumably that belonged to the woman. I felt with my foot and thrust my big toe right into a warm orifice. She giggled.

"That tickles," she said. She had continued to fondle me, long past the point where my sex could be in question, with the result that it was now bone hard and standing erect.

"I want to know what's the big idea, interrupting people like this," Henry said. "I've got a good mind to call the cops."

"I wouldn't," the woman said, changing positions so that she was lying alongside me. "Think of the publicity. Think of your wife. What if she read the papers?"

"I don't think she can even read," he said. "Say, whose side are you on, anyway?"

By this time she wasn't on her side at all, she was on her back, tugging ambitiously to get me on top of her. I offered some resistance, but, in the first place, I didn't realistically have much of an alternative. By this time the neighborhood was certainly crawling with cops, and I could hardly leave in my current state of undress. I needed a place to hole up, in a manner of speaking, and she was offering me one.

In the second place, I was somehow miraculously aroused. I suppose it was the result of the earlier excitement, the drinking and that wild chase on a fire truck. Whatever the cause, I was primed and ready. We managed to get into position and there was hardly any resistance when I slipped inside her.

"Henry, you're a rat," she said over my shoulder, wriggling happily in response to my deep thrust. "You didn't say anything about a wife to me."

"Must have neglected to mention it," Henry mumbled. "But, damn it, Doris, that's got nothing to do with his. We've been set upon by a madman. Heaven only knows what he intends to do with us."

"If he does to you what he's doing to me," she said, "You've got a streak in you I didn't suspect."

"What are you talking about?" There was some shuffling about and a hand moved along my leg, over my ass, and down to the point where Doris and I more or less became one. The hand felt my balls suspiciously.

"Thank you," I said.

"Doris!" The lights came on, blinding me. I blinked a few times before I got a good look at Doris. She wasn't all that bad—a little hard looking, but basically pretty. Henry was fat and bald and looked highly piqued at the situation.

"Hey, you look as good as you feel," Doris said, gazing appreciatively up at me. I had paused when the lights came on, not certain of Henry's reaction, but I figured if Doris did-

130

n't care what he saw, why should I? I took up my efforts again.

"What are you doing?" Henry demanded.

"You mean you can't tell from looking?" I asked. "Maybe I'm doing something wrong."

"You're doing everything just right," Doris said, beginning to pant a little.

"This is the limit," Henry said.

"Not far from it," I admitted, moving a little faster. I was rapidly approaching a climax, and from Doris's breathing and her increasingly frantic movements I felt pretty sure she was right along with me.

The doorbell rang. Doris seemed oblivious to the sound. "Aren't you going to answer that?" Henry asked.

"You get it," she said, clinging tightly to me.

Grunting angrily, Henry got up and walked to the door, his limp dick flopping ineffectually against his leg. As the door opened, I got a glimpse of men in blue.

"Ah hah," one of the policemen said, seizing Henry's arm. "You're just the guy we were looking for."

"What is this?" Henry asked, struggling to free himself from the grip. "What's this all about?"

"Don't give us that innocent routine," the officer said, holding firm. "We've been chasing your fire engine around town, and when we found it in the alley, we knew you had to be in this building. Come along now."

"There's some mistake," Henry said. "I've been here with my lady friend all evening."

"*Your* lady friend?" The cop looked past him to where Doris and I were still joined together. Caught in the act, so to speak, it seemed a bit pointless to try to hide what we were doing. I glanced back over my shoulder and waved to the officer with one hand.

"Don't mind us," Doris said, "We won't be long." To me, she asked, "Is that all of you?"

"I think so," I said, "Although with all these people around, we can't be sure."

"Do you know this guy, lady?" the officer asked, indicating Henry.

"Never saw him before in my life," Doris said without breaking rhythm. "My boyfriend and I were just spending a quiet evening together when that guy climbed in the window and dropped on top of us."

"Doris!" Henry was quite shocked. "This is preposterous," he told the policemen. "I've known this young lady nearly a year. We spend many evenings together, just like that."

"What a terrible thing to say," Doris said. "You ought to be ashamed of yourself, mister. Why, think how that would look if it came out in the papers. Think of what your wife would say."

"Certain grounds for divorce," I said, really pouring on the steam now. I could feel my climax welling up within me, ready to explode.

"And a fantastically expensive alimony," Doris added, writhing and thrashing wildly about. "Why, with a good lawyer, she could take you for every penny you have."

Henry looked completely nonplussed. "I've never had anything like this happen to me in my life," he said.

"Neither have I," said Doris. She sank her teeth into my shoulder and her body jerked spasmodically.

"Okay, buddy," the policeman said, "It's off to the station with you. You've got a lot of explaining to do." Two other policemen grabbed Henry and led forcibly from the room.

"Hey," another policeman said, for the first time getting a good look at Doris and me. "What are you doing?"

"Nothing, now," I said, letting out my breath in a long sigh. Doris' frantic climax had brought me off as well. "It's done."

I turned to look at the policeman still lingering in the door. "Would you fellows mind?" I said. "It's a little drafty in here."

# CHAPTER SEVENTEEN

I gave them a couple of long minutes before I got out of the bed. "Thanks for the help," I said.

"My pleasure," Doris replied, stretching contentedly. "Drop in anytime."

"I don't suppose you have anything in the way of men's clothing around the place?" I indicated my still naked body. "I sort of hesitate to go out like this."

"There's Henry's thing, but they wouldn't fit. And I think maybe there's a suit in the closet there."

There were, in fact, several changes of clothing, in varying sizes. "I take it Henry is not your only male friend," I said, finding a shirt in just my size.

"If you were a woman, would you be satisfied with Henry?" she asked.

"I wouldn't be satisfied with Henry regardless of what I was," I said. I found a pair of trousers and some loafers. Not a particularly chic outfit when I was done—brown loafers, black slacks, chartreuse shirt—but it would get me home, which was the important consideration.

"He pays the rent," she said with a shrug. "Or did. I don't suppose he'll do that any more."

"Sorry if I spoiled a good thing for you."

"One good thing deserves another," she said. "Look, you don't have to rush off, you know."

"Sorry," I said, smiling, "But I think I'd better, before Henry or the police return. Look, I'll send these things back to you, all right?"

"Not necessary. They none of them fit me anyway. Guys just sometimes leave things laying around, you know what I mean?"

I did, as a matter of fact, but I saw no particular reason to tell her my life story. "Well, thanks again," I said, going to the door. I peeked out cautiously. There was no one in sight. I waved and slipped out, closing the door after myself. I hoped Henry would be able to get out of his predicament.

\* \* \* \* \* \* \*

It was an easy matter to get a cab at the front door and in a short while I was back at my own apartment. The phone was ringing when I came in. It was Elliot.

"I was worried about you," he said. "I couldn't find a trace of you after the fire."

"I had, uh, some errands to run, so I sort of ducked out. How was the damage?"

"Very little, actually," he said. "It was a weird sort of fire—a lot of flames, but they actually didn't seem to burn much of anything. They were like artificial flames, almost, if you can figure that out."

I could. It was just like Lorin to end up producing flames that were more show than substance. Aloud, I said, "I'm glad nothing was harmed."

"Paul." He paused for a moment. "You know what I'm trying to do, don't you?"

"I'm not sure." That wasn't quite true. I had a pretty good idea.

"I want to win you back."

"You know what they say about rekindling an old fire," I said.

"This one never went out,' he said. "Not entirely. I never stopped caring for you and wanting you. You know that. And I think that somewhere inside, you still care for me."

"Maybe," I said. "Yes, surely. Frankly, right now I don't know where I stand on anything. I thought I did. I was all clear in my thinking, until…." I caught myself before I said, "Until Lorin came back." Instead, I said, "Until I started thinking about the past."

134

"Nobody can go back to the past, but we can learn from it. We can't just pretend it never was, which is what you've been trying to do."

The doorbell rang. "Look," I said, "When I've thought it all out, I promise I'll give you call, okay?"

"That's better than a flat turn-down," he said.

"I'm not so sure," I said, and hung up. I really did not know how I felt toward Elliot, or what I might do about him.

I still planned to marry Margo, and it seemed to me that it would be foolish to try to continue a relationship with someone who had once been a lover of mine. Sooner or later, sparks were bound to start flying.

On the other hand, if I were going to break off again with Elliot, it seemed cruel not to do so now, neatly, rather than holding out what might be a false hope to him.

Of course, that was the rub. I did not want to break off with Elliot again. I found myself thinking more and more of that past he had just mentioned. I remembered how I had enjoyed his company and how he had inspired me to make the most of myself and my talents. The truth was, I was awfully tempted by Elliot's proposal.

Lorin could not persuade me to give up my plans for going straight, despite all his appeal and his wiles. After all, no matter how you looked at it, Lorin was dead, and he was only back temporarily. Sooner or later, he would leave me, and I would be in limbo again.

Elliot, however, was alive and here and available, and the choice was no longer simply one of being tied to Lorin's memory, as I had been for too long, or going straight. There were other alternatives now.

At first, I didn't recognize the person at the door. He wore multi-colored pants, no shoes, a battered leather vest with tassels, and a prospector's hat. The floppy hat and magenta sunglasses hid a great deal of his face.

"Sorry," I said, starting to swing the door shut.

"Paul, it's me," Don said, taking off the sunglasses so I could see his eyes at least.

"For Pete's sake," I said, dragging him inside. "What are you doing in that get up?"

"I got it from a hippie on the Strip. He thought my dress was out of sight and wanted to trade. And I figured the police might be looking for the dress, so I got his costume instead."

"What happened to Lorin?" I asked.

Don shrugged, tossing his hat aside. "He just disappeared into the crowds. I haven't seen him since."

That was typical of Lorin—stir up all kinds of mischief and then, when the going got rough, save his own neck and to hell with anyone else.

"I don't know about you," I said, going toward the bar, "But I could stand a drink." It was nearly one thirty in the morning.

"Make that three," Lorin said, popping into view.

"You, damn you," I said, turning angrily on him.

"Now, darling, don't get in an uproar," he said, "All's well that ends well, remember?"

"We might have been arrested, or killed," I said.

"But we weren't. And it was fun, wasn't it?"

"No," I said gruffly.

"Actually, I thought it was groovy," Don said with a giggle.

"Darling boy," Lorin said, turning his charming smile on Don. "You know, there are still adventures waiting for you and me."

"I know," Don said enthusiastically, "Only, they'll have to wait until I come back from the country."

"From what country?" Lorin asked.

"My uncle—that's Margo's father—has invited some people down to the country for the weekend. I'll just get home in time to pack as it is."

"Good God," I said. "I completely forgot. I'm going too. I'm meeting Margo there."

Lorin looked thoughtfully from me to Don. "Well, in that case..." He snapped his fingers. A large suitcase, lipstick red, suddenly appeared beside him.

"What's that?" I asked warily.

He gave me a wide-eyed look. "You can't expect me to spend a weekend in the country with just what I'm wearing, can you?"

Since all that he was wearing was his birthday suit, it was a good point—but not, I thought, the central one. "You weren't invited," I said.

"Oversight," he said nonchalantly. "Excuse me, dears, I've got to make myself lovely."

He left us standing there and went gracefully up the stairs, humming "Yippe-ti-yi-a" as he went.

*THE GAY HAUNT*, BY VICTOR J. BANIS

# CHAPTER EIGHTEEN

It seemed as if I had just dropped off to sleep when the doorbell woke me. I came down in a robe, to discover Elliot standing outside. It was just about dawn. The sky behind him was starting to turn gray. I must have been in bed all of three or four hours.

"Elliot," I said, staring in astonishment. "What in God's name are you doing here at this hour?"

He swayed a little on his feet and I took his arm and brought him inside. My first thought was that he was sick, but one whiff of his breath explained the trouble.

"You're dead drunk," I said, steadying him.

He blinked and gave me a peculiar look. "Damned right," he said. "I got that way because I wanted to come over and see you."

"That's not particularly flattering," I said with a light laugh.

"Maybe not, but I for one am tired of flattering you."

I was surprised by his vehemence. He looked violently angry and quite unlike the Elliot I knew. "I think that's the whole trouble with us," he went on, jabbing a finger at me, "I've been too fucking nice, too namby pamby. I was good old Elliot, waiting around for you to wipe your shoes on him. No wonder you got bored."

"I didn't…" I started to say.

"So, I'm gonna show you I can be a man," he interrupted me. He grabbed me suddenly and gave me a rough kiss on the mouth. Notwithstanding his whisky breath and my lack of sleep, it was not altogether unpleasant.

"I always thought you were man enough," I said, a little uneasy at his strange behavior.

139

"You ain't seen nothin' yet," he said. Before I knew what he was doing, he had picked me up and thrown me over his shoulder.

"Hey, wait a minute," I objected, struggling to get back down, "I never liked this caveman routine."

"Fuck you," he said, carrying me toward the stairs.

It occurred to me that this was what he had in mind. I stopped struggling, for a variety of reasons. In the first place, there was damn little I could do. He was quite a bit bigger than I was, and as drunk as he was I didn't think I could count on his being gentle. In the second place, I found myself rather enjoying the situation.

When we got to my bedroom, he tossed me rather unceremoniously onto the bed. I hadn't even gotten my breath back before my clothes were being practically ripped off me. Somehow the possibility that I might ever be raped had seemed to me quite remote, but that was just about what was taking place—if you can call something that you are enjoying "rape."

This was a side I hadn't suspected existed in Elliot's makeup. It was rather a pleasant surprise, although, to be honest, I wasn't sure I could care for sex this way every day. For one thing, it would rapidly deplete one's wardrobe. By the time I was naked I had seen two buttons go flying across the room, heard a ripping sound that told me my shorts would not be wearable in the future, and had one zipper yanked irreparably out of shape.

I tried not to look too pleased with it all while Elliot hastily shed his clothes. He was better looking in the buff than I had remembered, lean and rangy and completely solid. No middle-age spread anywhere to be seen. His abdominal wall rippled with thick-ridged muscle. The shoulders were wide, the arms and legs muscular, the hips practically nonexistent. His cock, on the other hand, was very much existent, a long, thick headed rod that reminded me that Lorin had no monopoly on big dicks.

Carrying me upstairs and getting us both quickly out of our clothes hadn't cooled Elliot down any. I was surprised the bed survived the dive he took onto it, and me. I almost didn't.

140

I got a kiss, not one of those tender sentimental things I had gotten from him before, but a genuine damn-the-torpedoes-full-speed-ahead kiss that promised to leave my lips swollen and purple. He took a minute to bite each nipple, maybe a tad too fervently for comfort, and he sucked my cock—which was, needless to say, raring for action—into his mouth for a few, fast, clear-to-the-hilt slides.

Then my legs got hoisted rather rudely into the air over my head.

"Hey," I protested, suddenly enjoying it less, "That's not my route. You ought to remember that."

"My memory fails me," he said, spitting into his hand and smearing it across the swollen knob of his cock.

"Consider yourself reminded," I said, tensing as he thrust a moist finger into the tight opening.

"What are you going to do about it?" he challenged, holding my legs around his shoulders.

I started to say something, then stopped. It looked like there wasn't much I *could* do about it except relax and enjoy it. I tried relaxing. He smiled knowingly and withdrew his finger.

Relaxing enough to accommodate a finger, however, is a long way from relaxed enough to accommodate a big whang. He guided the head expertly to the opening and pushed. Nothing much happened. He pushed harder.

"I think we've got this whole thing wrong," I said, not intending a pun. "Why don't we talk it over?"

"I've got a better idea," he said. "Where's the Vaseline?"

"In the bathroom. But I don't think…."

"I do," he said, getting up and walking quickly to the bathroom. He was back in a flash. His cock looked bigger than before, and not too strangely, not nearly so pleasant as it had when he was undressing. It was also shiny with Vaseline.

There were no preliminaries this time. The legs went up. He found the mark. He shoved hard. My flesh yielded, albeit with reluctance, and I suddenly had that big head buried in my ass.

I let out a yelp and drew back, but in my position there wasn't much escape. He came with me, thrusting and going deeper. The tight channel was stretched wide. He pressed down, bending me almost double, and kissed me hard on the mouth, clasping my cock in his hand and beginning to work it up and down.

It still wasn't my cup of tea, but I decided it was kind of fun in a rough sort of way. It was inevitable anyway, so it would be foolish not to enjoy it. Besides, he must have been rubbing the prostate because all of a sudden I was hurting less and enjoying it more.

Of course, I wasn't going to give him the satisfaction of knowing that. "You son of a bitch," I grumbled when he finished the kiss.

"For someone who isn't enjoying it, you've got quite a boner," he said, rubbing his thumb lightly over the head where my cock had begun to exude a droplet of dew.

"Reflex," I said, thinking what a traitor the cock could be in certain situations. The truth was, I don't think Elliot gave a good rat's ass just then whether I was enjoying it or not.

He certainly wasn't making any effort to be gentle or tender. He had driven it home like a ramrod, and now he was fucking me with hard, wild strokes that sent his balls slapping against my upturned ass cheeks and took my breath away. The long, thick shaft slid in and out at a dizzying speed, and he seemed to kiss me and jerk my cock more to add to his own pleasure than to give me any.

I suppose he was punishing me for all the unhappiness I had caused him over the years. As punishments go, however, this one wasn't too bad. I wasn't sure that I'd be able to walk for the next few days, but I understood why some women wake up smiling. Painful or not, getting fucked gives you a filled up feeling impossible to get any other way. I decided to close me eyes and enjoy the experience.

It didn't last terribly long. Those deep, hard strokes brought Elliot to a fast climax. I recognized the change in his breathing and the sudden uneven rhythm to his fucking. He seemed to grow even larger inside me, shuddered once, and crammed everything he had into my sore butt.

142

I felt the splash of a particularly wild orgasm inside me. It triggered my own response. The rugged fuck I was getting and his continued hand motions had brought me to the peak as well, and the feel of his come spurting into me sent me over. I shot so suddenly and so violently it surprised even me, spraying both our bodies with the pearly liquid. Elliot sank down next to me, smearing my come between us.

I had a hollow feeling when he slipped out of me a minute later—and now that I had shot off, I was again aware of the fact that I was unaccustomed to taking it up the ass. I felt as though a freight train had driven through me. When I lowered my legs, an ache went all the way through me.

He gave my butt a smack and got up, striding wordlessly to the bathroom. I found a cigarette and lit it, puffing thoughtfully. He was back a few minutes later, smelling of a fresh shower, and began to don his clothes. He didn't say anything, although he glanced in my direction a couple of times.

When he was almost dressed, I decided I didn't like the frosty treatment. "Usually," I said, "They leave a couple of bucks on the dresser and say thanks."

"No thanks," he said, buttoning his shirt. "And no couple of bucks, either."

Finished dressing, he looked at me again. "Sore?" he asked.

"Yep."

"Mentally, or physically?"

"Both," I said.

"Good," he said, lighting a cigarette. "You needed some sense pounded into you."

"Where you were pounding is a long way from my brains," I said.

"Of the two, I think your ass knows more than your brains. Maybe you should start thinking with it instead. I have a feeling it would steer you right."

He went to the door and paused. "And I'm not apologizing, either," he said without turning. "You've had that coming for a long time, and I just decided to give it to you. After this, maybe you'll remember that I'm a man, not just some

toy for you to play around with when it suits your fancy."
With that he went out, slamming the door hard.

I got up and headed for the bathroom. He was certainly right about one thing: after this, I was sure to remember that he was a man.

My aching ass wouldn't let me forget.

# CHAPTER NINETEEN

The Sellers' ranch was nothing but an ultra luxurious house set out by itself on the fringe of the desert. There were no animals and no crops. So far as I could tell, nothing was produced there but suntans and hangovers. It was also a dreary place to spend a weekend, but I had seen so little of Margo lately that I knew I would be courting a major tantrum if I cancelled.

So, having recovered more or less from Elliot's coming, I loaded my things into the Jag and set out on the two hour drive that would take me there. Margo had gone down with her parents the night before.

I thought about calling Don and asking him to share the trip with me. He had said he was going, and I knew he didn't drive, but I decided against it. I didn't know how much, if anything, the family knew about his sexual habits but it might not look right for the two of us to arrive together, particularly since Margo had found him at my apartment on a recent morning.

I wasn't alone on the trip, of course, Lorin made his appearance soon after I started off. Presumably out of consideration for me, he wore clothing—and he made it clear that, although he had been out of sight, he had not been out of view range when Elliot had been at the apartment.

"That was quite a fuck you got this morning," he remarked, popping into view.

"Don't remind me," I said, shifting about slightly on the leather seat.

"I didn't think that one had it in him."

"It wasn't in him, it was in me."

"All the way, one might add," he said. "Too bad he's such a square. A man who can fuck like that could be a real treasure."

"He's not so square," I said. "He's not as wild as you are, I'll grant, but that isn't necessarily a bad thing, for your information."

"Pish," he said, "The next thing, you'll be thinking about accepting his proposal"

I didn't say anything. Arguing with Lorin was a futile exercise at best. I concentrated instead on driving. It was one of those days that makes California forgivable. There was no smog, the traffic was light, and not a cloud in the clear sky to interfere with the sun's golden rays. The wind rushing by gave me a sense of freedom. It was almost a shock when I reminded myself that my marriage to Margo was only two weeks away. I did not feel like a man on the verge of getting married.

I didn't realize I was grinning until Lorin asked, "What's funny?"

"Nothing, actually," I said. "I just feel good. I don't know what it is, but I feel ten years younger."

"A good fuck does that sometimes," he said.

"I don't think that's it exactly. I feel like, oh, I don't know. I feel like a kid who's fallen in love."

"Who are you in love with?" he asked sharply, looking across at me.

"No one," I said. "That is," I corrected myself quickly, "I'm in love with Margo, of course."

He grimaced. "Oh, her. I thought you'd forgotten about that."

"She'd never let me. If I wanted to forget, that is. Which I don't." I sounded irritable, I knew. It wasn't even Lorin with whom I was annoyed, but myself, because I had lied to him. For the first time, I had fully faced the fact that I did not love Margo. I was fond of her, of course, but I did not, and never had, loved her. Lorin had been right about that, although I did not want to tell him.

That did not necessarily mean I shouldn't marry her, however. Many very good marriages begin with nothing more than affection and mutual respect—so I had read. I

146

doubted that I would ever find a better wife for me than Margo. For the most part we got along well. If she did not give a great deal, neither did she ask much. Her demands were few, sufficiently so that I could adequately meet them.

She had compensating virtues as well. All right, it was true, her family was wealthy, and her father could do a great deal for my career. In a few years, I would be quite wealthy myself. I would never again have to worry about that sort of thing, and eventually, I would be able to devote some time to writing again. Strangely, Elliot had revived my interest in that.

I couldn't see that admitting I wasn't in love with Margo made such a change in things. So why, I asked myself, should I suddenly feel that I didn't want to get married?

\* \* \* \* \* \*

It was mid-afternoon by the time we arrived. I say "we," although Lorin was persuaded to drop out of sight just before I pulled into the drive.

The house was a big, arrogantly Western affair that sprawled around on several levels and managed to look completely unlike a ranch house. The front was overly land-scaped, brimming with cactus, palms, and cute little paths of stepping-stones that led nowhere. In back was a patio roughly the size of a football field, a pool almost as big, and a row of little dressing rooms decorated to look like Arabian tents—the brain child of Mrs. Sellers who no doubt felt like an houri when she entered one.

The interior of the house was Western in motif. Chande-liers looked like wagon wheels, vaguely early American so-fas and chairs were covered in what purported to be home-spun fabrics, at about fifty bucks per yard. It was the sort of house in which it was impossible to feel at ease. I had a dis-concerting vision of living years of my life in it, or some-thing very similar.

"Welcome to our little ranch," Mr. Sellers grunted when I came around the house with my bag. They were all at the pool: Mrs. Sellers looking a trifle too girlish in a fluffy dress, Margo stuffed into a bikini a size or two too small for her,

147

and Don, wearing what appeared to be a tiny handkerchief, cleverly folded.

Margo kissed me hello. "I've missed you," she said, with only a trace of sarcasm.

"I've missed you too," said dutifully "Look, I think I'll get into a swimming suit, too, and unpack these things while I'm at it."

"I'll show you your room," Margo said, getting up. It was hardly necessary. Every time I had been here I had used the same room, and I was certain that I would again. My hunch proved correct. I tossed my suitcase onto the chintz-covered bed and opened it.

"Aren't you forgetting something," Margo asked, standing at the foot of the bed.

"What's that?" I found my bathing suit and put it aside.

"You haven't said you love me."

"Of course I do," I said, not looking at her. The words sounded false even to my ears. "I love you," I said, more emphatically.

"Paul," she said, speaking slowly, "You know, we don't have to wait."

"For what?" I slipped my polo shirt over my head and tossed it on the bed. I had already kicked off my loafers and I started to unbuckle my belt, but for some reason, I suddenly felt uncomfortable about undressing in front of Margo.

"To get married," she said.

I told myself I was being silly, and opened my trousers, pushing them down and stepping out of them, but I still felt embarrassed about having my *fiancée* in the room. "Don't be silly," I said, "It's only two weeks."

"But that seems so far away," she said. "I can't explain it, exactly, it's just that…I feel as though that day will never come for us. I keep thinking we'll never be married. Paul, I want to elope, right away. We could go to Mexico and get one of those quickie marriages."

"What about the reception, and the plans your mother and you have made? Think of the money that's been spent." I turned my back on her while I peeled my shorts down and stepped out of them. I kept it turned while I put on the trunks.

"The money doesn't matter. Daddy has plenty. And we could go ahead with the reception. It doesn't have to be cancelled because we were married a few days early."

"People will think you're pregnant, rushing off and getting married in a hurry," I said, turning back now that I was covered. "Besides, you said it yourself, it's just a few days."

She looked so downhearted that I couldn't help taking her into my arms and kissing her comfortingly. "Look, you're just having bridal nerves," I told her, patting her shoulder. "When you start thinking about all the things that still have to be done, you'll wonder if two weeks is enough time to take care of it all."

"Oh, Paul, I feel so, so out of touch with you." She clung to me tightly. I ran my hand down her back, patting her buttons and felt her shiver. She wriggled against me hotly. "Let's do it," she whispered, nibbling my ear.

"Not right now," I said.

"Why not?"

I had to think of a reason. "Your parents might hear us. Or wonder why we're taking so long."

"They won't care. Anyway, I'm a big girl."

"And big girls can wait," I said, slapping her backside and freeing myself from her clinging grip. "Until tonight."

She pouted. "You promise? Tonight?"

"Tonight, I promise. Now, you go on down to the pool and I'll join you as soon as I finish unpacking."

She left reluctantly. I had only half finished putting my things away when someone tapped at the door.

"Come in," I called rather resignedly, thinking it was Margo returning.

It was Don, however. He didn't waste much time on conversation. "Hi," he said, coming straight across the room and into my arms to kiss me. I kissed him back for a full minute before I realized he had left the door open to the hall.

"Uh, excuse me," I said, letting him go while I went and closed it.

"I've been dying for you to get here," he said, hooking his thumbs in the elastic of his skimpy bathing suit and pulling it down. He stepped out of the suit and stood before me naked.

"Hey, wait," I said, unable to resist running my hands over his round little butt—so different, I thought, from Margo's.

"For what?" he said, looking surprised.

"For later." I pushed him away before my prick got any harder and started taking charge of the situation. "If I don't show up poolside very quickly, Margo will get suspicious and come back here looking for me. I don't think she would be happy to find us in a sixty-nine."

"I guess not," he sighed. He picked up his suit and stepped into it again. "Are you in love with Margo?"

"No," I admitted.

"Are you in love with me?"

"No."

His face brightened. "Goody, then we don't have to worry about anything getting sticky. I'll tell you what, I'll come to your room tonight after everyone's in bed. We can spend the whole night together."

I frowned thoughtfully. "Maybe I had better come to your room instead," I said. "Just to be safe."

"Okay." He came to me and stretched up to kiss me lightly before he left. I stared after him, wondering just how I was going to take care of both of them.

"You're going to be busy," Lorin said, appearing at my side.

"Yes," I agreed, putting my socks into a dresser drawer.

"I could take Don off your hands," he said.

"Thanks, but I think I'd just as soon handle that myself," I told him.

"Well, I'm not going to take care of *her* for you."

"Don't worry, I'll manage," I said, although I wasn't so sure. Of the two, I was most interested in making the scene with Don, and I felt pretty sure that after a bout with him, there would be nothing left for Margo. On the other hand, if I took care of Margo first, that would curtail somewhat my enjoyment of Don's wild little body.

So the obvious question was, how to put off Margo?

\* \* \* \* \* \* \*

150

By the time the day ended, I was no closer to a solution. We spent the afternoon swimming and lounging about the pool, and I pretended not to hear an occasional splash when there was no one to be seen swimming. Mrs. Sellers engaged me in some conversation which consisted mostly of how unselfishly she gave of her time to various charities and how this, in her mind, accounted for the fact that she remained so youthful.

"People often mistake Margo and me for sisters," she informed me.

I did not think it tactful to point out that, for one thing, Margo looked older than she was. In all fairness, Mrs. Sellers apparently had some rather young ideas. I caught her eyeing my body more than once. Presumably Mrs. Sellers no longer had the fuel to feed her furnace. I gave her my silent sympathy, but I had no intention of hauling the coal for her.

Dinner was on the patio as well—steaks from the grill with béarnaise sauce, a mountain of cold shrimp dishes, mushrooms stuffed with crabmeat. "Roughing it," as Mrs. Sellers put it. We washed it all down with champagne— Veuve Cliquot—and ended dinner with a velvety chocolate mousse. I felt like pioneer stock.

All that outdoor activity and the plentiful food offered one advantage: everyone was sleepy early. Or at least, they were ready for bed. We were still having coffee when Margo stood and stretched.

"I'm positively falling asleep," she said. "If everyone will excuse me, I think I'll turn in." She came across to my chair and leaned down to kiss me, giving my cheek a pinch. "Good night, darling," she said, looking so lewd that I expected a wink and a giggle. "Don't stay up too late."

"I won't," I promised. I had only one hope, that Margo might actually be sleepy enough from the swimming and heavy dinner to fall asleep. When she had gone in, I helped myself to more coffee and a brandy from the tray Mr. Sellers had produced. The best thing I could do, I thought, was give her plenty of time.

Don was the next to go, soon after. He rose and stretched and said, "I think Margo's right. Guess I'll call it quits too. Night, all." He waved to the group in general and to me a little more particularly, and tripped inside.

"Fine young man," I said when he was gone.

"Humph," Mr. Sellers grunted. "Sissy, if you ask me."

"But such a sweet young thing," Mrs. Sellers said. "He's such a help when he's around. He helps me with the decorating, picks clothes, styles my hair. There's nothing he can't do."

I thought of several possibilities, but left them unspoken. Instead. I had some more brandy. The Sellers began to fidget after a bit. They were waiting, I guessed, for me to decide to retire. I sipped my brandy and repeatedly fought back the urge to yawn.

They lasted slightly more than an hour. Mr. Sellers finally gave up the attempt at courtesy. "Sorry to be a party-pooper," he said, getting up, "But it's time I called it a day. You two stay out here as long as you like."

I caught a glimpse of a flicker in Mrs. Sellers' eyes and decided perhaps Margo had had time enough to fall asleep. "I think I'm due to retire too," I said, standing up.

"No need to hurry off," Mrs. Sellers said with a too-bright smile. "We can sit out here in the moonlight as long as you like."

"Sounds pleasant, but I'm afraid you'd soon be listening to me snore," I said.

She looked disappointed, but held out her hand for me to help her up. When I did, she managed to brush against me, which I pretended not to notice.

In my own room, I undressed and turned out the lights. I lit a cigarette and sat by the window watching the twinkling of the stars while I waited for everyone except—I hoped—Don to fall asleep.

I finally decided that I had waited long enough. The house was still. I put on a robe and slipped into the hall. I had to pause to get my bearings. I knew Margo's room was at the opposite end of the wing, around the corner and down another hall from mine. Her parents' rooms were here with mine, as was the other guest room where I presumed Don to be.

Just across the hall and down a few feet, a door was slightly ajar. Don, it seemed, was waiting for me. I went swiftly and silently to the door and pushed it open, stealing into the room before anybody came along to see me.

"Still awake?" I whispered into the darkness.

"Um hum," was the sleeping sounding answer. That didn't worry me, though. I had ways of waking him up. I felt my way in the direction of his voice. The room was black except for a thin line that shone from beneath one door, apparently the bathroom.

I bumped into the bed and reached out to feel my way around to the side. I touched a foot, and pinched one toe playfully, feeling my way up the leg to guide me around the bed. I felt an ankle, a calf, and then the hem of a silk nightgown.

"What are you doing wearing a nightgown?" I asked, reaching up under it to grope him.

"I always wear a nightgown to bed, silly," Mrs. Sellers said. I felt an opening where Don's cock should have been. She sighed and parted her legs. "I knew you'd come to me tonight," she said. "I just felt it in my bones."

I yanked my hand away and pulled her nightgown back down over her legs. "Sorry," I said, standing. "There must be a mistake. Wrong bone."

"Darling boy," she whispered after me. I hurried back toward the door, banging my shins on a chair. "Damn," I swore, hopping around on one leg.

I found the hall door again and opened it quietly. After one quick glance, however, I ducked back inside and pulled the door closed. Margo was just outside and a few feet along the hall, at my door. Even if I had wanted to see her, I didn't want her to see me coming out of her mother's bedroom.

I followed the direction of the light under the other door. I remembered that this room was at a corner of the hall. If the bathroom had a hall door, it would open around the corner, where Margo wouldn't see me.

What I forgot in my anxiety was that the bathroom connected Mrs. Sellers' bedroom with that of her husband. I stepped into the lighted bathroom, closing the door after myself, and turned around to find myself staring down into Mr.

153

Sellers' face. Staring down, not because he was particularly short, but because he was seated.

He bent forward, putting his hands over his crotch—an unnecessary gesture, since anything that might have been there was amply covered by rolls of flesh—and gave me a startled look.

"What are you doing here?" he demanded. It was surprising how less dignified the man looked and even sounded when on the john. "And what were you doing in my wife's bedroom?"

"I was looking for a bathroom," I said.

"There's one in your own room," he pointed out, holding his knees tightly together.

"I didn't like the color," I said. "Excuse me, I'll come back when you're finished." I went by him with a nod and a smile, into his bedroom. It was dark here too, but I managed to find the hall door.

Unfortunately, Margo had apparently given up on my room and was en route back to her own. She paused as I opened the door of her father's room and, afraid she might look back, I closed it again.

Mr. Sellers was still seated when I came back through the bathroom. "Pardon me," I said, walking hastily.

"Not at all," he said coldly. "On your next visit, bring a couple of beers with you and we'll discuss the current market situation."

"I knew you'd come back to me," Mrs. Sellers whispered as I closed the bathroom door.

"Please, your husband' right beyond that door," I said, felling my way toward the hall.

"He's on the toilet, isn't he?"

"Yes."

"Then we've got a good hour to ourselves," she said.

"Good," I said, reaching the door and opening it cautiously. The coast was clear and I stole into the hall. "See you around," I said, and closed the door to her room.

The other room had to be Don's. I went there and tapped lightly. There was no answer, so I opened the door and poked my head in. "Still awake?" I asked.

154

He still didn't answer. I stepped inside and held the door open to let a little light in. His bed was empty.

"Damn," I said to myself. Probably he had gotten tired of waiting and gone off somewhere. Maybe he was even with Lorin.

I stepped into the hall again just in time to see Mrs. Sellers enter my room, closing the door after herself. I paused in the hall and scratched my head, trying to figure out the latest score in our game of musical beds. Margo was in her room by now. Mrs. Sellers was in my room. Don was nowhere to be seen, and Mr. Sellers was on the john. And I, for one, was getting sleepy.

"To hell with it," I said. I returned to Mrs. Sellers' room and crawled into her bed. The brandy and all that fresh air earlier were beginning to tell. Later I would worry about trying to straighten things out. For now, I felt like a little nap. I dropped off in minutes.

Sometimes after I fell asleep I began to dream. Don was with me, or possibly Lorin. No, it was Elliot. He was in bed with me, close enough that I could feel his warmth. He grunted as he turned over and put a hand on my hip, running it down and over the curve of my ass.

"You asleep, dear?" Mr. Sellers asked, intruding on my dreams.

"Um hum," I murmured in my sleep, pushing back against his hand and wriggling my butt.

It didn't soak into my consciousness until the overhead light flicked on, bringing me wide awake. Margo was in the doorway.

"Daddy!" she said, staring in amazement at Mr. Sellers and me, in bed together. "Paul! What are you two doing in here?"

Mr. Sellers and I sat up together, equally shocked. "What are you doing here?" Mr. Sellers demanded. "And where is my wife?"

"She's in his room," Margo wailed, pointing. "With my cousin, Don!"

# *THE GAY HAUNT*, BY VICTOR J. BANIS

# CHAPTER TWENTY

I left early in the morning, after a fast cup of coffee. None of the family was around and I was certain the atmosphere would be a little chilly when they did make an appearance, so I left a note for Margo and packed my things. Don joined me before I left.

"You might as well give me a lift," he said when he saw that I was leaving. "I think the weekend is shot."

We were both quiet and rather morose on the trip back. There was no traffic out this early on Sunday and I drove fast. It was only mid-morning when we reached the city.

I had almost forgotten Lorin in my dejected mood. He did not appear until we were just a few blocks from Don's apartment.

"Hello," Don greeted him.

"Hi," Lorin said. "What a gloomy crowd. Aren't you two ever going to smile again?"

"What's to smile about?" Don asked. "I probably just got disinherited. As mad as my uncle and aunt were, I might even have to get a job or something."

"That is depressing," Lorin agreed.

"I'll probably be looking for one myself," I said, parking in front of Don's apartment building.

"Come on, let's have Bloody Marys," Don said.

I shrugged and climbed out. I didn't have much of anything else to do. Inside, Don and I sat glumly in chairs while Lorin took charge of fixing us drinks. He didn't have to look around to find the liquor.

"Cheer up," he said, handing us each a tall glass.

"Nothing would cheer me up," Don said.

"When I used to get depressed," Lorin said, "I always had sex."

Don looked less gloomy. "Does it work?"

"It always did for me."

"Okay," Don said, suddenly radiant again. "We were going to get together anyway, remember?"

"I remember," Lorin said, setting his drink aside.

"Count me out," I said, sipping my drink. I was a little disappointed that they didn't try to coax me. They started kissing and it seemed after a minute or two as if they had forgotten I was there, which did not exactly brighten my mood.

"If no one minds, I think I'll leave," I said, finishing my drink. No one minded. No one noticed. I let myself out and went back to my car.

I had breakfast at a dingy little coffee shop and drove to Griffith Park and the zoo there. I spent several hours walking about, looking at the animals and thinking, but I was no closer to a decision when I left than when I arrived.

I had scarcely gotten home before the doorbell rang. I answered it to find both Margo and her father there. I had a hunch that Mr. Sellers wasn't just along for the ride.

"About last night...." I started to apologize.

Mr. Sellers raised a hand to stop me. "Don't even attempt an explanation," he said, "I'd as soon forget that any of it even happened."

There was an awkward pause. "Drink, anyone?" I suggested. "How about a Bloody Mary?"

"Sissy drink," Mr. Sellers mumbled.

"I don't care to drink so early, you know," Margo said. She seated herself primly on the sofa while her father deposited his considerable bulk in my favorite chair.

"Well, if you don't mind, I'll have one," I said, going behind the bar.

"Papa and I have come to a decision," Margo said, making it sound like a major announcement.

"Which is?" I had a pretty good idea, but this was her show and I didn't want to spoil it for her.

"That we should get married at once," she said.

158

"You and your father?" I asked, looking up while I stirred the tomato juice. "Isn't that illegal, not to mention somewhat immoral?"

"Young man," Mr. Sellers said, flushing. "There is nothing at all wrong with *my* morals. My daughter refers to the oft-discussed but still unconsummated marriage between you and she."

"I should hardly think, as a father, you would want it consummated before the wedding takes place," I remarked. I saw no point in telling him that our relationship was about as consummated as it would ever get.

"I'm not interested in arguing the niceties of the language with you," he puffed, his face getting redder with each remark. "What I am interested in is whether you agree to marry my daughter at once, with no more of these silly delays?"

"Isn't that something Margo and I should be discussing? These days, that isn't usually settled between the groom and the father."

"Daddy is speaking for me," Margo said. She stood and came to the bar, clasping my free hand in both of hers. "Oh, darling, I just want to have an end to all this nonsense. I know you love me. You do, don't you?"

"Yes, although I guess not in the conventional sense of the word."

She smiled and nodded. "Oh, I know, you just aren't conventional, and I am, but I do love you, and I want to marry you, and I want that now."

In a way, I felt sorry for Margo. Instinctively, she knew how mismatched we were. Maybe she had even sensed it before I did, but she was willing to kid herself and me and her father, and the whole world if necessary. I wondered as I looked away from her pleading expression, whether she really loved me as much as she thought she did, or if I were only her last, ever-so-faint hope of escape from what, even to her, must be a monotonous life.

"And you father is here to enforce your wishes, is that the idea?' I asked.

She took her hands slowly from mine. "I don't think *enforce* has a very nice ring to it," she said.

"Should it have?" I looked past her to her father, who glowered steadily at me from his chair. "Let me ask a question. What happens if I don't agree to this hurry-up marriage? What if I say I want to wait a while longer?"

Mr. Sellers cleared his throat, which meant he was about to deliver remarks that had been well rehearsed in advance. "That might be a little awkward," he said. "There's the question of your partnership. I'd like to get that settled at the next board meeting, which is next Tuesday."

"And that depends upon my marrying Margo? Right away, you mean?" He said nothing. I turned to her. "Margo?"

She looked away. "That's rather a humiliating question," she said in a tiny voice.

"For both of us," I said.

Mr. Sellers got abruptly to his feet. "I think, my dear," he addressed Margo, "That we are wasting our time here. I think, young man, that you should spend an hour or two in serious thought."

"Paul," Margo said, her back turned to me, "You don't want to marry me just now, do you?"

"No," I said. I was surprised at how easily, without any pause for reflection, I made that decision. Until then I had dreaded her question, knowing I'd be forced into deciding, but when it came, it was no more than a snap of the fingers.

"Or ever?" she added, in a still smaller voice.

"Or ever," I said.

There were tears in her eyes when she turned back, but my answer was the honest one. Any other answer would have been cheating both of us and just storing up unhappiness for later.

"Margo," I said, trying to smile at her, "I'm gay."

It had been a long time since I had made that statement to anybody—to myself, especially—but suddenly I knew that was honest, too, and all my posturing to the contrary had been sham.

"But, Paul," she said, "I want you to be happy."

"Dear, naïve Margo," I said, shaking my head, "What I'm saying is that I am...homosexual is the politest term, I guess."

"I don't understand," Mr. Sellers said, looking both be-wildered and indignant at this turn of events. "What are you trying to tell us?"

"It's not so difficult to understand," I said to him a bit impatiently. "I suck cock. Does that make it clearer?"

He drew himself up with all the dignity that he could muster, which was admittedly quite a bit. "Margo, it's time we were going," he said, taking her arm firmly and propel-ling her toward the door. When he got there, he turned back to me to say, "There'll be no need for you to give the matter any further thought. I'll have Miss Byrd send your things to you."

Margo gave me one last, incredulous look, and then they were gone. For a moment I stood in silence, looking after them. Then, because I suddenly felt freer than I had in years, I threw back my head and laughed, hard.

I was still laughing when Elliot answered his phone. "What's with you?" he asked. "You sound like you've got a feather stuck up your ass."

I laughed even harder. "How'd you like to replace it with something else?"

"I didn't think you liked it that way," he said, a trifle cautiously. He probably thought I was drunk.

"From here on in, I like it every way," I said. "Anyway and anywhere *you* want to stick it."

"Anywhere I want?" He paused for a moment. "Is this by any chance a proposal?"

"No," I said, "It's an answer to your proposal."

"Do you really mean…?"

"I calculate," I said, glancing at my watch, "That in the time we've already talked, you could have reached your car and started over here."

"Get rid of the feather," he said with a low chuckle. "I'm on my way."

I took the stairs two at a time and probably set a couple of world records for showering, shaving, perfuming and dressing again. In practically no time at all, I was back downstairs at the bar. I started to mix another Bloody Mary, thought *what the hell*, and brought out a bottle of champagne instead. Today was a special day if there ever was one.

Lorin and Don appeared just about the time the cork popped. "What's the occasion?" Lorin asked. "Pour us some."

"By all means," I said, filling three glasses. "You'll want to celebrate this with me. I just told Margo—and her father—to go fly a kite."

"Heaven, I'll drink to that," Lorin said.

"Poor Margo," Don said.

We toasted one another with our glasses and drank. "I suppose," Lorin said, wrinkling his nose, "This just means it's going to be you and Elliot again?"

"How did you guess?"

"Easy, it was all over your face the other day when you went to see him again after all these years."

"Hell, I didn't even know it then myself," I said.

"You just didn't want to face it." He lifted his glass again. "Well, at least you're back in the fold, so my trip wasn't wasted."

"Then you're going back?" I asked. I felt a strange mixture of relief and sadness.

He sighed and grinned. "Have to. They're giving me all kinds of signals. Anyway, Don can't stay more than a few minutes."

"Don?" I nearly choked on my champagne. For the first time, it soaked into my consciousness that they had arrived together, just approaching out of nowhere, both naked. Only ghosts could do that, to the best of my knowledge.

I turned frightened eyes on the pretty young man next to Lorin. "Are you....?"

He nodded at my alarm. "Um hum," he said.

"But you were always...human," I objected.

"Oh, I just turned spirit," he said. "Didn't you hear the sirens?"

"Sirens?" I shook my head. "What happened?"

"Well...we had tried practically everything," he said, giggling. "Lorin is so groovy. He had a few ideas I hadn't even heard of, and that doesn't happen often."

"You're no amateur yourself," Lorin said, beaming at him.

162

"So," Don said, speaking to me again, "We were just sort of playing around, and Lorin said, why didn't we have it in front of the fireplace, so I thought that was a great idea, and I lit the gas fireplace. Only, it didn't come on."

"We were busy again by that time," Lorin said, "And we didn't notice that the pilot was off. Pretty soon we were doing a sixty-nine and had forgotten all about the gas coming out of that thing."

"Didn't you notice the odor?" I asked, shocked to imagine the scene.

Lorin shrugged. "His apartment is right on the street. I thought a Volkswagen had farted."

"Anyway," Don said, "Something ignited the gas after a while."

"I think we were making sparks," Lorin said.

"And here we are," Don concluded. "It was a spectacular blast, I must say. They're already talking maybe it was anarchists and that sort of thing."

"But, don't you...don't you feel bad about just, just going like that?" I asked, not sure of the protocol with someone so recently deceased.

He smiled and shook his head, reaching to take one of Lorin's hands in his. "No, Lorin's been telling me all about what it's like over there, and it sounds just groovy. And we'll be together forever, if we want."

"In that case," I said, draining my glass, "I wish you the best. If *you* don't mind, there's no reason for me to."

"And when you get there," Lorin said, "We're going to try that threesome. Don thinks it's a grand idea, too."

"Do me a favor," I said, pointing the bottle at him, "Don't do anything to speed it up. I've just started living this life again. Give me some time to enjoy it."

"Oops," Don said, and with that he was gone. "Lorin," he called from somewhere distant.

"Go ahead," Lorin called back, "I'll catch up with you, don't worry."

He turned to me and I was surprised to see that he looked sad. "It has to be goodbye, Paul," he said. "I'm beginning to fade already."

"Will you come back again?" I asked. I was even more surprised to discover how sad I felt. It was not easy, losing someone twice that you cared about. I thought I had cried all my tears for Lorin five years before, but now there were some leftovers filling up my eyes.

"Not for another hundred years," he said. "That's the rule, anyway."

We both grinned. Lorin, of course, would always find some way of breaking the rules if he felt so inclined—but the message was clear. The past was dead and buried, more so than Lorin.

I took him in my arms and kissed him—rather quickly, because he really was starting to fade now. I could see daylight through one of his arms, and his lips were like the brush of a feather against mine.

He stepped back, and I could see right through him. Still he lingered. "I really did love you, darling," he said, his voice like the sigh of the wind. "Not just more than any of the others, but differently."

"I understand," I said. "My feelings for you were unique, too."

"You were the only thing in this whole world that I missed when I left it," he said. I thought he blew me a kiss, but he was too pale now to see clearly, and in another second he was gone altogether.

"Lorin," I called after him, not certain whether he was still close enough to hear me. "No one will ever take the place that you held in my heart. No matter how we quarreled, you'll always have a place there."

The doorbell shattered the melancholy mood that had settled over me. I had completely forgotten that Elliot was on his way. Remembering, though, I was glad all over again. I went to the door with a smile on my lips.

He hardly waited for the door to close before he grabbed me and kissed me, long and hard. I listened and heard my heart singing, and knew that it was right. This would be no madcap adventure, no roller coaster ride. Life with Elliot would never contain that kind of excitement, but I knew that with him I would enjoy something that would never have been possible with Lorin.

The thought of Lorin made me suddenly aware of something odd. Elliot had one arm about me, that hand on my shoulder, and the other hand on my waist—but there was yet another hand touching me, its fingers playfully mussing the hair at the back of my neck. I grinned inwardly. It was like Lorin to hang around until the last possible second. I wondered what the penalties were for being A.W.O.L. from wherever he was stationed.

Something whispered in my ear, so faintly I could almost believe I had imagined it. "I loved you, you big jerk." Sentiment had never been Lorin's forte.

"I loved you too," I whispered back.

Elliot lifted his face and looked down at me. "Why did you use the past tense?" he asked.

"Because I did love you," I said, "And still do, and will tomorrow. And forever."

"Bad form for a writer," he said. "Forever isn't possible, unless you believe in life after death."

"I believe in forever," I said, inviting another kiss.

He almost kissed me and then remembered something. "Too?" he asked.

"Hmm?"

"You said, 'I loved you too.' But I hadn't said that I loved you."

I took hold of his face with both hands and brought it down to mine.

"Then," I said, just before our mouths came together again, "Isn't it about time you got with it?"

Lorin presumably was gone completely by now, but I couldn't swear to it. He might have been screaming at the top of his lungs just then, and I wouldn't have heard him.

*THE GAY HAUNT*, BY VICTOR J. BANIS

THE GAY HAUNT, BY VICTOR J. BANIS

## AFTERWORD

I wrote *The Gay Haunt* in 1970. In 2005, my long time friend and editor, Earl Kemp, who now edits an online zine, *eI*, ask me if I would write an article for his zine on legendary publisher Maurice Girodias (The Olympia Press, The Other Traveller).

Since my only experience with Mister Girodias was with the publication of this novel, the article I wrote for Earl was perforce about *The Gay Haunt*.

I thought that it might be instructive to include it here, and I do so as it appeared in *eI*, including the Author's note, and with the kind permission of Mister Kemp and *eI*:

*Author's note: It will be helpful here to explain a little about my history. I began my writing career in sexy paperbacks, euphemistically called pulps today and which are, to my great surprise, highly collectible now. Although I was a self-described "paperback virgin" when I began, naïve and unsophisticated in the sexual ways of the world, I learned quickly—purely, you understand, as an academic exercise. I mostly enjoyed myself and as I saw it, was paid (often very good money) to practice my writing craft. The proper business of the writer is writing; like any language, the more you practice the language of writing, the more fluent you become at it. For the beginning writer, that often means trying to squeeze in time before and after the work day to ply his trade; so it is a plus if the neophyte writer can find someone to pay him to put words on paper. I was happy to do so. I learned a lot about writing, and especially, the discipline of writing, by turning out all those pulp novels.*

*By 1970, however, the pulp field had shrunk, both in terms of production and money paid to writers. Fortunately, by this time I had already moved on, and I was writing gothic thrillers and historical fiction. I no longer had any particular interest in writing the sexy gay novels that had been the mainstay of my career theretofore and which I now thought a closed chapter in my past; then, unexpectedly, I was approached by Maurice Girodias, of Olympia Press in Paris, who published important but out-of-the-mainstream works by such authors as Henry Miller, Anaïs Nin and Vladimir Nabokov. To those of us who fought in the Free Speech battles of the sixties and seventies, Girodias and his Olympia Press were the stuff of legend. Needless to say, I was flattered and easily convinced to revisit my gay pulp roots. That adventure, or misadventure, as it might be considered, is chronicled below.*

## A VIRGIN ANEW

By the year 1970, my virginity was a moldy relic of the past; and I had sadly learned that the world neither little wants nor long remembers moldy virginity. I had more than a hundred books under my belt by this time; yes, it is true, most of them well below my belt. I had been in and out of more beds than Fanny Hill. I had been down in the valley and over the hump. I had sported boots and heels high and low, and some of them round. I had wrestled with issues large and slippery, inched my way into places dark and perilous, sometimes groping my way blindly. With my hand in Old McDonald's, I had trotted with turkeys, wallowed with

168

swine, and milked the cows, so to speak. I had lollopped with lesbians, strummed with studs, and fiddled with fags. I'd had my nose, at least, in everything but Jack Horner's pie, and if the little bugger had stayed in the corner where he belonged, I'd have tales to tell you about those plums too. I was the Czar of the bizarre, the Queen of the *Kamasutra*, Orifice Rex.

Then, *un bel di* (I always try to slip a little foreign tongue in where I can) I looked across the vast wasteland of my mattress—ignoring the scorch marks here and there—and asked myself the age old question: Is that all there is?

"Face it, sweetie," my Muse replied (This was Snotto, the Muse of Sleaze; they sometimes leave her out of the artier books), "At the banquet of life, you're down to licking the plates."

I took a moment to consider that. It was true. Plus, my tongue was tired. The time had come, it seemed, to get out of bed.

I swapped my scarlet swaddling for a nightgown of white purity, scrubbed the rouge from my face, poked a judicious hairpin here and there, and gazed into the mirror. Jan Alexander, Mistress of the Frightened Virgins, smiled back at me. Hmm. If I kept the lights low enough, no one would suspect it was I.

Ring went the phone. Ring, ring, ring, ring—I was sitting in pitch darkness, as you recall. I groped my way to it, and found my agent, Jay Garon, at hand.

"Maurice Girodias wants you," Jay announced, and added, "Do you know the name?"

Maurice Girodias? In our war for freedom of speech, he was the Commander in Chief on the French battlefield. Olympia Press. The Traveller's Companion. The elite of erotica: Miller, Nin, Nabokov. Like visions of sugarplums, they danced in my hair-pinned head. *Of course I knew that name.*

What was truly surprising, be still my heart, was that he knew *my* name. He had read, in fact, some of what I had written for Greenleaf Classics—in particular, the C.A.M.P. series. Now, he was about to launch a new American line of paperback erotica, The Other Traveller, and, oh, joy, he specifically wanted me to write a book for this new imprint.

Jay really flattered me when he said, "Girodias said he thinks of you as being a star of the Greenleaf stable. He asked which other Greenleaf writers I represent and if I could get them to write for him."

"He really said that?" I asked.

At last, a man who wanted me as I was. I was a virgin again. Off came that nightie—white makes me look sallow anyway—out came the hairpins, and on went the lipstick. I flung myself upon the bed—carefully covering the scorch marks as best I could with splayed limbs—and crooned those titillating words into the phone: "How much is the gentleman going to pay for my services?"

"Fifteen hundred dollars," Jay crooned back.

Fifteen hundred? I pulled the sheet up to my chin. "But, Jay, darling," I said, "I am an ardent believer in tit for tat, and I am getting a great deal more tat than that from my frightened virgins."

"Think of the prestige," Jay countered.

I carefully opened a package of prestige, poured some into a Tupperware bowl, and considered it long and carefully. Well, I suppose I could eat that if it came down to it. God knows I had eaten almost everything else, though sometimes under duress.

"And, he's offering a generous royalty," he added.

I said yes, but with a teensy bit less enthusiasm than before. I couldn't help thinking my virginity was being taken a trifle lightly. I should perhaps have remembered what a wise old man once told me (actually, it was Lady Agatha, but there wasn't much that girl didn't know about men): "If the handwriting on the wall starts out, 'for a good time, call...' hold off on ordering the bridal bouquet."

Well, still, this was Maurice Girodias, the big hollyhock in our garden and I a lowly pansy. And where the bee sucks, there suck I. Besides, it says in the Bible—or it might be one of Martha Stewart's books, I get them confused—if you are going to say yes to a consummation, you might as well throw your body and soul into it. Let's be frank: after some of the places I had tossed my body, this was kid's stuff to me. In

170

less than a month, and with a brief kiss blown in Thorne Smith's direction, I had completed *The Gay Haunt* and sent it off to Jay. I prettied myself up and waited for the wedding night. I don't care how many times you do it in the back seat of a car, it doesn't count until you've checked into a motel. I was still a virgin.

An eager virgin, I might say. By then, I had gotten the contract for the book, and Jay was right, the royalties were generous: twelve percent for the first 50,000 copies, which was the first print run; fourteen percent for the next 50,000; and sixteen percent for anything over that. The fifteen hundred dollars in advance wasn't much, it was true, but if the book sold even most of its first, fifty thousand printing—and most of my gay novels had easily topped those numbers—I could look forward to a big fat check by springtime. A pleasure delayed is sometimes all the more thrilling when it finally comes off.

In the meantime, though, there was the matter of that fifteen hundred dollars in advance; which was no longer technically "in advance," since they had the manuscript and I had nothing to show for my virginity but a lot of promises on paper. I know that there are those who have said I sold myself cheaply, but I have always insisted on something more than hot air (admittedly, that can add to certain kinds of fun, but at the moment I was alone in my boudoir with a bad case of financus interruptus).

I splashed myself with Oh Dick Alone and called Jay Garon. "Where," I asked, "is my fifteen hundred?"

He called Mister Girodias and called me back: "Next week, he promises."

The following week, I rearranged the bed sheets prettily and called Jay Garon. "Where," I asked, "is my fifteen hundred?"

He called Mister Girodias and called me back: "Two weeks, he promises."

Two weeks passed. I repaired my mascara, painted my toenails—yes, Jungle Red—and called Jay: "Where," I asked….

Well, to make a sad story short, I did indeed get the fifteen hundred dollars, but not before my Avon lady had driven off in a brand new Cadillac; and, more tellingly, not until the book was on the racks, sporting that familiar green cover and looking, I had to admit, plenty classy. Not exactly kosher, it seemed to me, but, let's be realistic, once you have your hot hands on what you wanted so desperately, it's easy to forgive all that hard-to-get business that went before.

Besides, I could understand, I thought. Setting up a new business, in a new country: of course, it must be complicated and costly. At least now, however, the books were out there, which meant money was coming in. My royalties would surely be simpler to collect. This was, after all, Maurice Girodias. If you couldn't trust a hollyhock, whom could you trust?

Nor was there any question that there must be royalties, because in no time at all, that original edition had been replaced with a second printing, and a different cover: sexier, if a trifle less classy looking. Which meant that the book had already sold out its initial fifty thousand copies. At a twelve percent royalty, that check I was expecting would be very fat indeed. Let them laugh who will, not everyone gets a big fat one for their virginity.

My royalty statement came at last. I ripped the envelope open, and took out: a single sheet of paper. I shook it, shook the envelope, tore it seam from seam searching for the enclosed check. There was none. I returned my attention to the royalty statement, and saw that the book had sold a mere five thousand copies. It hadn't even, according to the royalty statement, earned back that paltry "advance," which in any case had been more of an "after."

"There must be some mistake," I wailed to Jay. "They've lost a zero, and I want it back."

He called Mister Girodias and called me again: "Book tallies are slow. It's a new operation. Wait for the next royalty statement. Oh, and he would love to have another book."

Well, yes, wasn't that like, "come again on the tapioca?" My wedding night was still unconsummated and we were talking another round of foreplay.

I replied that I would wait for that next royalty statement before I started another book. Six months to wait, then. A long time to lie breathlessly on your mattress waiting for what you want to come. Still, what was coming was also growing larger, always a happy state of affairs, it seemed to me. Before those six months had passed, the second edition of *The Gay Haunt* had been replaced on the racks by a third, with still another cover, and that edition, too, was flying out of the stores. One hundred thousand copies at least, then, and the second half of that was earning a fourteen percent royalty. I began to shop for a new peignoir and called my delighted Avon lady again, who mentioned that she thought the new Mercedes model was quite handsome.

The next royalty statement arrived. The book had now sold, it said, somewhere around ten thousand copies. I slipped back into my old chenille bathrobe, dabbed some Old Spice behind my ears, and called Jay. The Other Traveller, it seemed to me, was traveling by alleys and devious routes.

Jay agreed. He called Mister Girodias—who wasn't in, it seemed, but would call back.

He didn't. Jay called again. Mister Girodias was once again out of his office, but he would call back.

He didn't. And so it went for several weeks, while I restocked my makeup cabinet and waved to my Avon lady, who was as pleased as punch with her new Mercedes.

\* \* \* \* \* \* \*

I never got that royalty payment. Not a sou. The Other Traveller folded. Girodias, I was told, had returned to Paris where, no doubt, he was happily cavorting with the money he hadn't paid me. I had been plucked. Royally. By a hollyhock.

I took another look at that Tupperware bowl. It wasn't prestige in there, after all, it was baloney. I knew that Maurice Girodias looked down his nose at the California pulp publishers, but I had worked with those people for years and found them gentlemen and ladies one and all (sometimes one and the same), for whom a handshake constituted a contract and one's word was bond; ironically amusing, then, to learn the true meaning of the word "sleaze."

Well, I had learned a valuable lesson or two from it all: first, get the money and stick it in your garter before you roll down your panties. Also, save the makeup for the morning after, I don't care what your Avon lady advises.

These may seem minor points to you, but it is just such wisdom as this that has guided me down the sometimes-circuitous pathways and through the meadows of my life.

Plus, I still had that original book with its classy green cover, and the two other editions with their different covers, and I discovered, when I reread it long after, that it was a very funny book; so I was glad to have written it and to have it on the shelf, and delighted when, years later, Michael Bronski included an excerpt in his *Pulp Friction*. All in all, I think it's one of the better things I did, which is to say, the experience can't be considered a total loss.

Besides, I was a virgin again.

## ABOUT THE AUTHOR

*Lecturer, former writing instructor and early rabble-rouser for gay rights and freedom of the press,* **VICTOR J. BANIS** *is the critically acclaimed author ("...a master storyteller"—* Publishers Weekly*) of more than 140 published novels and nonfiction works, and his verse and short pieces have appeared in numerous journals (*Blithe House Quarterly, *Fall 2006) and anthologies (*Charmed Lives, Lethe Press, 2006*).*

www.ingramcontent.com/pod-product-compliance
Lightning Source LLC
Chambersburg PA
CBHW051917240626
47153CB00004B/1265